Nobody's Daughter

NOBODY'S ✛ DAUGHTER

Susan Beth Pfeffer

A YEARLING BOOK

Published by
Bantam Doubleday Dell Books for Young Readers
a division of
Bantam Doubleday Dell Publishing Group, Inc.
1540 Broadway
New York, New York 10036

ISBN: 0-440-41160-2

Reprinted by arrangement with Delacorte Press

Printed in the United States of America

April 1996

10 9 8 7 6 5 4 3 2 1

OPM

✦ Chapter 1

"Poor child."

Emily Lathrop Hasbrouck looked around to see which one of her great-aunt Mabel's well-meaning friends had said that. It didn't matter really which one had. They all had murmured it in the past three days since her aunt's death. "What's to become of her?" someone else whispered.

Emily was unable to make out the reply. Aunt Mabel's friends were all happy enough to let her hear about her pitiful condition, but not especially eager to tell her what her future was going to be.

"It was a beautiful day for a funeral," one of the women said. "Just the sort of day Mabel would have wished for."

"A saint," another woman said. "Taking that child in and providing her with a home."

"And now what's to become of her?"

"Hello, Emily."

Emily looked over and saw Mrs. James, her piano teacher, entering the parlor. "Hello, Mrs. James," she said.

"You've been very brave," Mrs. James said. "I'm sure your aunt would have been quite proud of you."

"Thank you, ma'am," Emily said.

"I can't help thinking of your mother," Mrs. James said. "You were such a little thing when she died. Do you remember her at all?"

Emily shook her head. She did have faint memories of a beautiful lady holding her close, but she was never sure whether the memories were real or a dream. Either way they were too personal to share, even with Mrs. James, who had always been quite kind to her.

Mrs. James took Emily's hand. They left the front parlor, where everybody was sitting around, and went to the dining room. "Has anyone discussed with you where you're going to live now?" she asked.

"No, ma'am," Emily said. "Have you heard anything?"

"I'm afraid not," Mrs. James said. "Whatever does happen, Emily, I want you to promise that you'll keep on with the piano. You have a gift for music, and it would be a pity if you stopped playing now."

"I hope I can keep on with it," Emily said. "I guess it depends where I go."

"It's what your aunt would have wanted for you," Mrs. James said. "She truly enjoyed your playing. Even after she got sick and you had to leave school, she insisted you keep on with your piano lessons."

"That's because we're Lathrops," Emily said. "Aunt Mabel always said Lathrops are musically inclined." In fact, Emily first learned how to play the piano from her father, but she'd never mentioned that to Aunt Mabel. Hasbroucks were no-accounts, and no-accounts weren't supposed to be musical like Lathrops.

"Your mother was a wonderful musician," Mrs. James said. "We took piano lessons from the same teacher when we were girls. I look at you, Emily, and I see a lot of her."

Emily smiled. She loved hearing things about her mother. She rarely had been able to get a nice word about her mother from her aunt. Then she stopped smiling, in case you weren't supposed to smile after a funeral.

Aunt Mabel and Emily had lived alone, so everyone had gathered at the Reverend Mr. Dowling's house following the funeral. Mr. Dowling was the minister at the Methodist church, and he had been a good friend of Aunt Mabel's. If anybody knew what was going to become of Emily, she was sure it was he.

"I have to be going home," Mrs. James said. "My husband is unwell. I wish I could take you in, but it simply would not be possible, Emily. You do understand, don't you?"

"Of course," Emily said. She never expected Mrs. James, or anybody else in Madison, to take her in. The only reason Aunt Mabel had was because she was kin.

Mrs. James looked at Emily. Emily half expected her to say, "You poor child," but she didn't. Instead she bent down and kissed Emily on her forehead. "God will watch out for you," she said. "Be a good girl and work hard and make something of yourself. Make your mother proud."

"Yes, Mrs. James," Emily said. She walked with the piano teacher to the front door and watched as she left. Emily felt more alone then than she had since her father had died, and that was four years ago.

She felt no hurry to go back into the parlor and deal with Aunt Mabel's friends. Instead she stood in the hallway and listened to what they were saying. "Little pitchers have big ears," Aunt Mabel had been fond of saying, although Emily had rarely been guilty of eavesdropping on her aunt. There'd been no need to. The older Aunt Mabel had grown, the louder her voice had become.

"Where will the poor child go?" Emily overheard someone asking.

"I'm sure Mabel made arrangements for her," someone else said.

"What about her sister? Do you think Emily will go live with her?"

Sister? What sister? Emily asked herself. Did Aunt Mabel have a sister? Emily was sure she would have been told. Aunt Mabel was always talking about the Lathrops and what a fine upstanding family they were, in comparison to the Hasbroucks, Emily's father's family. The Hasbroucks were, without exception, derelicts and sinners.

"You mean that little baby?" someone asked. "How could Emily go live with her?"

"She must be eight by now."

"What little sister?" someone else asked.

Emily pressed her ear to the wall, to be sure she could make out every word of the answer.

"Jane Hasbrouck died in childbirth, when Emily was three. She had a baby girl. Naturally that drunkard husband of hers didn't want to have anything to do with the baby."

"What became of it?"

"Someone took her. Mabel never spoke about it, but I'm sure it was a respectable family."

"Emily can't stay with her sister, if no one knows where that sister is."

"No, I suppose not."

"It was just like that George Hasbrouck to give away a helpless baby to strangers. A drunkard and a ne'er-do-well."

"Shush. Judge not . . ."

"Where is the poor child?"

The poor child in question tried to catch her breath. Emily had known her mother had died in

5

childbirth, but had assumed the baby had died as well. Now that she thought about it, no one had ever actually told her that. It was just that the baby was never spoken about, not even at those times when her father had grown maudlin and cried over the memory of his beloved lost wife.

A sister. Emily could scarcely believe it. She had a sister. She wasn't alone after all. Somewhere she had a sister, a baby sister. An eight-year-old girl, half Lathrop, half Hasbrouck, just the same as her.

"Poor Emily."

"Poor child indeed. You don't suppose she'll be sent to a city asylum?"

"I don't know what else might become of her."

"How ironic."

"Whatever do you mean, Dorothy?"

"Emily in one of those wretched asylums, while her sister is brought up by good Christian folk. It was Emily who tended to Mabel these past months."

"That was her Christian duty. Mabel took that child in and gave her food and shelter. Her father was white trash, and her mother went against family wishes when she married him. Mabel Lathrop was a saint to have given the girl as much as she did."

"Quiet, Bertha. It's hardly the child's fault that her father was a Hasbrouck. And Emily is a good girl."

"What a shame if she should be placed in a city

6

asylum. Elsie and I brought Christmas gifts to the children at one of those homes once, and we were just appalled at the conditions. The children might almost have been better off on the streets."

"Why, Emily. What are you doing there?"

"Oh, hello, Reverend Dowling," Emily said. She hadn't heard the minister leave his office and walk into the hallway. She was sure he knew what she had been doing. Reverend Dowling always seemed to know everything sinful she did. He'd had many conversations with Aunt Mabel on that very subject.

But this time the minister didn't look as though he was going to scold her. "Why don't you come with me to my office," he said. "There are things I need to tell you."

"Yes, sir," Emily said. She left her comfortable spot by the parlor and followed the minister to his office. She'd spent a lot of time in that room, when she'd first moved in with Aunt Mabel. Her aunt had been healthy then, and frequently brought Emily to the minister's house. While Aunt Mabel and Mrs. Dowling had tea, Emily had been given Bible lessons about sin and temptation.

"Sit down, child," Mr. Dowling said.

Emily sat in the chair by the minister's desk. It made her nervous that he was using the same tone that all of Aunt Mabel's friends had employed around her.

"Mrs. Dowling and I were talking about you just this morning," he said. "We agreed that in the four years you had the good fortune to live with your aunt, you have become a fine, well-behaved girl."

Emily wasn't sure how she was supposed to respond to a compliment, so she kept silent.

"Mabel Lathrop was a true Christian woman," Mr. Dowling declared. "She never wanted to take you in, you know. But when your father died, she felt it was her duty to do so. There were no other Lathrops who could take on the responsibility, and of course the Hasbroucks could scarcely be trusted with you. Had it not been for your great-aunt, you undoubtedly would have been placed in an asylum upon your father's unfortunate demise."

Emily thought about mentioning her baby sister, who was growing up with a family somewhere, but knew better than to say anything. Undoubtedly Reverend Dowling knew all about the baby sister, and if he had been unwilling all these years to tell Emily about her, it was hardly Emily's place to bring her up now. But still, she couldn't help wondering if such a home might not have been found for her. Aunt Mabel had taken her in because she was kin, and Emily had naturally assumed only kin took in kin. But apparently strangers did as well.

"I'm sure you're concerned about what your future will be," Mr. Dowling said. "If you were just a bit older, we could have found a place for you as a servant in some good home. Mrs. Dowling was commenting to me about what a good housemaid you would be. Mabel clearly saw to it that you mastered all the domestic arts. Mrs. Dowling said, and I concur, that it was always a pleasure to visit Mabel's house, even these past few months, because everything was so tidy. Mabel Lathrop truly believed that cleanliness was next to godliness, and her good influence can be seen in how well you tended her home."

"Yes, sir," Emily said. In spite of herself, she felt a wave of resentment that she had been forced to leave school and spend her days caring for her aunt and her aunt's house. Emily knew Aunt Mabel didn't have to take her in, and it was the least that Emily could do, in repayment for her aunt's many acts of kindness and generosity, to sacrifice her own pleasures for Aunt Mabel's care. But she had so liked going to school. True, Aunt Mabel had continued teaching her. But at school, there were children Emily's age, and the occasional chance to play. Once Aunt Mabel had become bedridden, all that was lost.

Emily reminded herself that Aunt Mabel had allowed her to continue with her piano lessons, and with her practicing as well. Emily knew she was sinful to want so much, school and friends and piano lessons. It was undoubtedly the Hasbrouck in her to be so greedy.

"But you're too young to go into service," Mr. Dowling said. Emily was startled by the interruption to her thoughts. She'd been thinking about herself rather than paying attention to her elders.

Another sin she was guilty of. "And between you and me, I don't think Mabel Lathrop would have approved of any kin of hers in service anyway. If there was one sin that good woman could be found guilty of, it was that of pride. So perhaps it's for the best that you're too young for such employment."

Emily blushed, thinking of the long list of sins she was guilty of. Pride was was just one of them. Not that she had any cause to be proud, being half Hasbrouck. She supposed it was the Lathrop in her that was relieved to learn she was too young to become a housemaid.

Mr. Dowling coughed. "Your aunt Mabel made no provisions for you," he said. "I suppose she felt she had done all she was required to by taking you in and providing you with a good home in her lifetime. She was not a wealthy woman, and what small estate she had she chose not to leave to you. She told me once that she dreaded the thought that any Hasbrouck should own any of her belongings, and she did not except you from that. It was Mabel's firm conviction that your mother's marriage to George Hasbrouck shortened the life of Jeremiah Lathrop. Mabel's beloved brother. Your grandfather. Mabel was too good a woman to hold that against you, but nonetheless she chose not to make you a beneficiary in her will."

Emily had never thought about Aunt Mabel's will before. She wasn't surprised to learn she'd inherited nothing. Aunt Mabel had certainly never promised her anything.

"Of course, that leaves you a penniless orphan," Mr. Dowling said, "as you were upon your father's untimely demise. But then you had a great-aunt to take you in. And now you have nobody."

Emily nodded.

"Under ordinary circumstances a girl of your age with no money and no family would be sent to one of the orphan asylums in the city," Mr. Dowling continued. "It would be a sad fate for a child such as you, who has known the blessing of a good Christian home. The orphanages in the city are forced to take in any manner of child. Ruffians, immigrants, the poorest of the poor are given shelter there. And frankly, such orphanages are fearful places. I served on a committee overseeing one such place a few years ago, and it was terrible indeed. But if that was God's will, then you should be grateful to be given a bed there, and not be forced to live on the streets, begging for food."

"Yes, sir," Emily whispered.

The minister smiled. "But God once again has shown you mercy," he declared. "One of the members of our parish knows a member of the board of trustees of the Mary Louise Austen Home for Orphaned Girls. It's an excellent home, located in Oakbridge, about sixty miles from here. I telephoned Miss Browne, who runs the home, the day after your poor aunt Mabel's death, and Miss

Browne at first said they couldn't possibly take you in. They never accept girls over the age of twelve, and of course your twelfth birthday is just a few months away. But the board member spoke to her, and Miss Browne was persuaded to change her mind. Mrs. Dowling and I will make the trip with you to Oakbridge tomorrow."

"Thank you, sir," Emily said.

"From what I hear, the Austen Home is quite well run," Mr. Dowling said. "I've never been there, but it's my understanding that the wards there are well fed and tended. Of course, being an orphanage, they are forced to take in all manner of girls, but once there, each one is given a proper moral upbringing. You will have the opportunity to resume your schooling, which your poor aunt's unfortunate illness caused to be interrupted."

"Do they have a piano?" Emily asked. She knew children should be seen and not heard, but she felt she had to know that. She only hoped Reverend Dowling would forgive her for asking such a question.

"A girl in your circumstances should be grateful for what she receives," the minister said. "You'll be given a roof over your head, three meals a day, decent clothing, and the opportunity to receive an education. You should thank God for that much, and not wish for anything more, Emily."

"Yes, sir," Emily said. She knew she'd been guilty once again of the sin of covetousness. Reverend Dowling was right. She could easily have ended up in a city asylum or on the streets, and instead she was going to be sent to the Austen Home.

But she knew it was only temporary. Now that she'd discovered she had a sister, Emily was sure her stay at the Austen Home, at any Home, would be only until she could find her kin and become part of her family.

⊷ Chapter 2

Emily sat patiently at Miss Browne's desk and waited for her new life at the Austen Home to begin.

She noticed that the room she was in had a sense of order and calm. She liked that. Outside the room, she could hear the noise of children's voices, as well as those of adults scolding or prodding those children along. But the room she was in seemed designed to keep those noises out. It had heavy drapes and thick carpets. The desk was old but smelled of polish. The chair Emily sat in was overstuffed and comfortable. There were group pictures on the walls, large assemblages of children. Emily would have liked to look at the pictures, but she wasn't sure she was allowed. She remained in the chair.

There were file cabinets in the room, made of

the same heavy dark wood as the desk. Emily had seen file cabinets at the doctor's office where she used to go with Aunt Mabel before her aunt had gotten so ill that the doctor came to their house instead. Emily wondered about the file cabinets. Were they filled with the stories of the girls whose pictures decorated the walls? Of all the questions Emily was wondering about, that was the least frightening one, so she allowed herself to ask it again and again. Then she wondered if her own story was already in the file cabinet, or whether it was on the desk in front of her. Maybe her sister's name was right in front of her, waiting for Emily to learn.

Emily sat up straight and practiced her fingering. She didn't think the Austen Home had a piano, but maybe, just maybe it did. And even if it didn't, she was sure her sister's house had one. Her sister was undoubtedly musical, and the people who were raising her, her parents, had to have noticed and bought her a piano.

Emily's left leg itched. She was all alone in the office, and the drapes were drawn, so no one could look in. She checked around carefully anyway, and then allowed herself the pleasure of scratching. Ladies didn't scratch. Ladies never itched so there was no need. The very fact that she had itched proved conclusively to Emily that she was far more a Hasbrouck than a Lathrop.

Emily wondered if her sister's family knew about the Hasbroucks, or whether they thought the baby they took in was somehow all Lathrop. She hoped they wouldn't hold it against her that she bore the Hasbrouck name.

She thought about her father then. She'd been thinking about him a lot since Aunt Mabel had died. She could remember his playing the piano, and the way he'd sit at the kitchen table and cry. She could even remember the sound of his laughter, and the way he used to tell her that she was all he had in the world. He might have been a Hasbrouck, but Emily knew that he'd loved her.

Emily's leg itched again. She was just about to scratch it when she heard the door open behind her. In walked a lady Emily assumed was Miss Browne. Emily stood up, the way Aunt Mabel had taught her to do.

The lady smiled and told Emily to sit down. Emily did. The lady didn't look mean, which was a comfort. Aunt Mabel had told Emily plenty of times how lucky she was to be the recipient of charity from a family member and not from an institution.

"You must be Emily Hasbrouck," the lady said.

"Yes, ma'am," Emily said. "Emily Lathrop Hasbrouck."

"I'm Miss Browne," the lady said. "I run the Mary Louise Austen Home for Orphaned Girls." She smiled again. "We call it the Austen Home for short. You are now an Austen girl."

"Yes, ma'am. Thank you, ma'am."

"I spent much of this morning speaking to people who knew your aunt," Miss Browne said. "Her doctor and her lawyer, and of course, Mr. Dowling. I wanted to find out as much about you as I possibly could before you arrived."

"Yes, ma'am," Emily said.

"They tell me your mother died when you were quite young," Miss Browne said. "And your father died a few years after that. And then you lived with your aunt."

"My great-aunt, ma'am," Emily said.

"Your great-aunt," Miss Browne said. She didn't seem to mind that Emily had corrected her. "Your mother's aunt, was she?"

"Yes, ma'am," Emily said.

"Your great-aunt's lawyer didn't know of any family members on your father's side," Miss Browne said.

"No, ma'am," Emily said. "My father always told me he didn't have much of a family."

"And I gather what few relatives your aunt had left were unable or unwilling to take you in," Miss Browne said. "From what your great-aunt's lawyer told me, you were quite fortunate that your great-aunt took you in at all. She must have been a very kindly woman."

"Yes, ma'am," Emily said.

"I'm sure you miss her a great deal," Miss Browne said. "Were the two of you quite close?"

"We spent a lot of time together," Emily said.

Miss Browne smiled at her. "What kinds of things did you do together?" she asked.

"Aunt Mabel taught me things," Emily replied. "She taught me more than I ever learned in school. So when she got so sick, I didn't have to go to school anymore. I could stay home and take care of her."

"That must have been lonely for you," Miss Browne said. "Did you get to play with other children?"

"No, ma'am," Emily said. "I played with children when I was little, before my father died. But not after Aunt Mabel took me in. So I didn't miss it when she took ill."

"Did your aunt Mabel like a quiet house?" Miss Browne asked.

"Oh, yes, ma'am," Emily said. "But she let me play the piano. There was a piano in my father's house, and I learned how to play there, and then after he died and I moved in with Aunt Mabel she let me have piano lessons. Even when she got sick, she let me keep on my lessons and practice. She liked it best when I played her favorite hymns, but she let me play other things as well."

"That was very kind of her," Miss Browne said.

"Yes, ma'am, it was," Emily replied. "I don't suppose you have a piano here?"

"I'm afraid not," Miss Browne said. "We'd like for our girls to learn the finer things, but of course we're dependent on the charity of others even for the food we eat and the clothes we wear. A piano is a little too much to hope for." She smiled at Emily, so Emily smiled back.

"Besides," Miss Browne said. "Things might get noisy if we had a piano. And we try to keep things as quiet as possible because there are so many girls living here. Now that you're an Austen girl, I'm sure you'll appreciate how quiet we keep the Home."

"Yes, ma'am," Emily said.

"We have four dormitories," Miss Browne said. "One for infants, and one for young children. Then there's a dormitory for girls eight to twelve, and another for girls twelve to sixteen. It's most unusual for us to take a girl as close to twelve as you, since all our girls leave when they're sixteen if we haven't been able to place them before then."

"Yes, ma'am," Emily said. "How do girls get placed?"

"We find homes for some of our girls," Miss Browne said. "Of course, the younger the girl, the more likely she is to be adopted. But on occasion a family will be looking for an older girl to help them out with their younger children, as a sort of a nursery maid. And of course some girls go to live with relatives or even return to their own parents. Not all our girls are orphans. Some are half-orphans, but their mothers or fathers simply can't afford to raise them. And let me assure you, if you do stay with us until you're sixteen, by the time you leave you'll be well trained in the domestic arts. We place many of our girls as servants in the finest homes. Others go to work in the mill. There's a quarry outside of town, and many of the girls marry men who work there."

Emily thought about what her aunt Mabel would have said to that. Lathrops, she was sure, were never supposed to be servants, or mill hands, or the wives of quarrymen. "I have family," she said. "I have a sister." Just saying it aloud excited her.

"Yes," Miss Browne said. She poked around her desk, looking for a piece of paper. Emily wished she could see just what was written on the paper, but the desk was too big and the handwriting too small. "Your mother died in 1905 in childbirth. She had a baby girl."

"Yes, ma'am," Emily said. Until Miss Browne said it, Emily hadn't been sure it was true. She could hardly contain her pleasure.

"Your great-aunt's lawyer told me that the baby was adopted by a family right after your mother's death," Miss Browne said. "Have you seen her since then?"

"No, ma'am," Emily replied. "But she's my sister anyway. She's my family."

"It's good to have family," Miss Browne said. "But as many of the girls here know, sometimes your family can't look after you. And you can hardly expect a little girl to take care of you now."

"No, ma'am," Emily said. "But I do have a sister. I do have family."

"Do you know where she is?" Miss Browne asked.

Emily shook her head.

"Do you know the name of the family that adopted her?"

Emily shook her head again.

"Do you even know your sister's first name?" Miss Browne asked.

"No, ma'am," Emily said. "But she's my sister anyway. I do have family."

Miss Browne sighed. "I don't wish to be harsh," she said. "But if you had family that was willing to take you in, you wouldn't be here right now. We never encourage our girls to have unrealistic fantasies about what life would be like for them out there. It only encourages them to run away, and make dreadful mistakes that could ruin their lives."

"Yes, ma'am," Emily said. Aunt Mabel had told her many times about dreadful mistakes. Emily's mother had made many of them by marrying a Hasbrouck.

"Right now you live in the Austen Home for Orphaned Girls," Miss Browne said. "And you'll continue to live here until we can find a family willing to take you in or until you're sixteen and old enough to be out on your own. This is a good home. You'll never be cold or go hungry. You'll go to school in town with children from fine families. You'll be taught sewing and ironing and other skills you'll be able to use when you do leave here.

If you're a good girl and obey our rules, you'll find life here comfortable, and the years will go by swiftly."

"Yes, ma'am," Emily said.

"But if you persist in fantasies about your sister, or some other family member you haven't even met, then the years here will be painful," Miss Browne said. "Believe me, Emily, I'm telling you this for your own good. It's the girls who long for something else who are the most unhappy. The ones who accept their lot with good cheer find much to be grateful for at the Austen Home."

"Yes, ma'am," Emily said.

"Now it's obvious your great-aunt brought you up in a proper Christian household," Miss Browne said. "You have good manners and a respectful way about you. No doubt you'll make friends and do well here. And before you know it, you'll be sixteen and ready to assume your place in life."

"Yes, ma'am," Emily said.

Miss Browne smiled at Emily again. She sure smiled more than Aunt Mabel ever had, but the words she said weren't all that different.

"We're going to place you in the older girls' dormitory," she said. "You'd be moving there in a few months anyway. Matron will show you where the dormitory is, but you'll be spending a few days in the isolation room first. We can't take any chances that you might be bringing an infectious disease here. When one girl gets sick, they all do."

"I'm not sick, ma'am," Emily said.

"I'm sure you're not," Miss Browne said. "But sometimes a girl can feel perfectly healthy and the next day she can have the measles or the mumps. We always keep our new girls isolated for the first few days just to make sure. And Matron will cut your hair off as well."

"She will?" Emily asked. "Aunt Mabel let me have braids just as long as I took care of them. I can take care of my hair, honest, Miss Browne."

"I'm sure you can, Emily," Miss Browne said. "And when your hair grows out, if you want you can wear it in braids. We don't dictate hairstyles for our older girls. But so many girls come to us with head lice that we have to cut off their hair before they move into the dormitories. Your hair will grow out again before you know it."

"Yes, ma'am," Emily said. Before she knew it, she'd be out of isolation and have her braids again and be sixteen and ready for employment as a domestic servant. She could hardly wait for "before she knew it" to begin.

✦ Chapter 3

"How bad do I look?" Emily asked the next Monday as she walked to school with two other girls from her dormitory.

"You look okay," Gracie Dodge said. "Really, you're very pretty."

"You look like a plucked chicken," Mary Kate Smith said. "All new girls do until their hair grows out."

Emily sighed. Aunt Mabel hadn't approved of mirrors, claiming that vanity was an easy first step to damnation, and the orphan home didn't have a lot of mirrors either. But she didn't see how she could look very good, what with her hair all chopped off. Her new outfit didn't help. All the Austen girls wore the same uniform, a dull blue dress with an oversized collar. The clothes Emily had brought with her from Aunt Mabel's had been taken away, in case they carried fleas or other vermin. Aunt Mabel hadn't been one for pretty dresses, but even so Emily missed having her own wardrobe. The idea of wearing the same dress six days a week for the next four years really depressed her.

"What's school like here?" she asked Gracie and Mary Kate. The two girls had the beds nearest hers in the dormitory. Gracie was twelve and Mary Kate thirteen, and they'd both lived in the Home for years. Most of the girls in the dormitory were fourteen or younger. It seemed that once you turned fourteen, you were a lot more likely to be placed with a family as a domestic or to run away. Running away seemed like a fine idea to Emily, but she wasn't sure she wanted to wait until she was fourteen.

"School's nice," Gracie said. "I like it."

"School stinks," Mary Kate said. "It's even worse than the Home."

Emily smiled. It hadn't taken her long to discover that Gracie saw the best in everything and Mary Kate the worst.

"Mary Kate, you're always saying such bad things," Gracie declared. "This is Emily's first day at school. Give her a chance. Maybe she'll like it."

Mary Kate shook her head. "She'll hate it," she said. "She hates everything else."

"That's not true," Gracie said. "Is it, Emily?"

Emily thought about it. She'd hated being kept in isolation, but compared to living in a dormitory with twenty strangers and just a narrow bed and a couple of pegs to hang your clothes on to call your own, isolation was a pleasure. She hated having no hair. She hated the uniforms. She missed playing the piano. And the quiet Miss Browne had promised was simply a way of saying that the girls weren't supposed to talk during mealtimes or while walking in the halls or before going to bed. But somehow there was a lot of noise anyway.

She didn't have as much physical work to do in the orphan home as she had with Aunt Mabel, that was true. Each girl was assigned a task, and Emily's was to help set the tables for breakfast and clear the dishes afterward. Not a great job, but nothing like what she had been doing. But Emily had never minded working. It gave her something to do during those last long days of her aunt's illness. So even that wasn't a real improvement.

"Do you hate everything?" Gracie asked.

"I don't know yet," Emily replied. "But I don't much like things."

"You'll hate things soon enough," Mary Kate said.

"You'll like school," Gracie said. "School's fun. I like reading and history the best."

Emily was looking forward to school. She'd missed going the past year, even though Aunt Mabel had been an excellent teacher and Emily had kept up with her classwork. She'd never had a lot of friends at school, because she'd always been expected to go straight home after classes were over, except for the days she'd had piano lessons. But she'd enjoyed even the little contact she'd had with children her age.

"What won't I like about school?" she asked Mary Kate. Mary Kate was the one to ask about things, since she hated everything and knew what to warn you about.

"Mary Kate just doesn't like school," Gracie said. "She never has."

"School's boring," Mary Kate said. "I hate being cooped up in a classroom."

"Is that all?" Emily asked. She'd had years of experience being cooped up. That she could handle.

"No," Mary Kate said. "That's not all."

Even Gracie looked uncomfortable. "What is it?" Emily asked. "What's bad about school?"

"It's the kids from town," Mary Kate said. "The way they treat us."

"Maybe they'll be nicer to Emily," Gracie said. "Maybe they're mean to us because we've lived in the orphan home for so long. Maybe when they see Emily's a new girl, they won't make fun of her."

"I hate them," Mary Kate said. "The way they look down their noses at us. Like we asked to live in an orphan asylum. I didn't ask to be a foundling."

"It's terrible being a foundling," Gracie said to Emily. "I don't know that from personal experience, of course, since I have a mother and she'll be coming to get me just as soon as she can."

Mary Kate snorted.

"She will be," Gracie said. "She told me so."

"She told you so when you were six," Mary Kate said. "You've been waiting six years, Gracie."

"I'm sure she's been too busy," Gracie said. "I know my mother loves me and wants me with her. But poor Mary Kate doesn't know who her people are. That's a terrible burden to bear."

"You don't know anything about them?" Emily asked.

"I know enough," Mary Kate said.

"They left a note with her," Gracie said. "When Mary Kate was just a little baby, they left her at the orphan home's door, all wrapped up in a blanket, and there was a note."

"What did the note say?" Emily asked.

"It said her name was Mary Kate and they should please take very good care of her," Gracie replied.

"It said more than that," Mary Kate said. "I know because I read the note."

"You have it?" Emily asked.

"No, it's in Miss Browne's file cabinets," Mary Kate said. "All the information about us is in those cabinets. But I snuck down there one night and read my file. And the note was there. It was from my mother. It said she wished she could keep me but she couldn't because the man she loved had

28

done her wrong and it turned out he was married to somebody else."

"Mary Kate's illegitimate," Gracie said. "It's a terrible burden being illegitimate, although I wouldn't know from personal experience."

"A lot of people won't adopt you if you're illegitimate," Mary Kate said. "If she hadn't left the note, nobody would know."

"It wasn't very thoughtful of her," Gracie said. "Leaving a note like that, and not even bothering to write down what Mary Kate's last name really was."

"If she'd said what my name was, they would have found her," Mary Kate said. "She would have gotten into trouble for leaving me there. That's why she didn't write my name down."

"The orphan home named her Smith," Gracie said. "They didn't have to give me a new last name, because I came with one, since my parents were married and my mother didn't just leave me at the steps wrapped up in a blanket."

"What happened to your father?" Emily asked.

"I don't really know," Gracie said. "But I'm sure he died very respectably."

Mary Kate rolled her eyes. "She's probably illegitimate too," she said. "A lot of the half-orphans in the home are, but their mothers lie about it."

"You take that back, Mary Kate No-Last-Name!" Gracie said. "I had a real father and he and my mama were married and loved each other very much. Just the same as Emily's parents. Right, Emily?"

"My parents were married," Emily said. "I guess they loved each other. I don't remember my mama very much."

"I don't care," Mary Kate said. "When I run away from the orphan home, I'm going to give myself a whole new name. I'm going to go on the stage and rich men will give me diamonds and furs."

"What about you, Gracie?" Emily asked. "What are you going to do?"

"After my mama takes me home?" Gracie asked. "I suppose I'll stay with her until I find some fine young man to marry. Then I'll have lots and lots of babies and be a wonderful wife and mother. What do you want to do, Emily?"

Before Emily had a chance to answer, three girls approached her and her friends.

"Look at this," one of the girls said. "It's a brand-new hog."

"A real ugly one, too," the second girl said. "She's the baldest hog I ever saw."

"Here, piggy, piggy, piggy," the third girl called out.

"She isn't a pig," the first girl said. "She's a hog. Pigs have breeding. Pigs are smart. Hogs are just dirty stupid animals."

"Ignore them," Gracie said. "They're mean. Everybody knows that."

"Hog, hog, hog," one of the girls said.

"Why are you calling me that?" Emily asked.

"It stands for Home for Orphaned Girls," Mary Kate said. "HOG. They think it's funny."

"The hogs can speak," the first girl said. She was taller than the others and had on a middy dress. "Listen up, everybody. We have talking hogs. Bald, ugly, stupid, talking hogs."

"Most hogs just grunt," the second girl said. "You know, oink, oink."

"Pigs go oink," the girl in the middy said. "Hogs just roll around in the mud." She pushed Emily down onto the street and roared with laughter.

"You stop that!" Mary Kate shouted, kicking the girl in the shin.

"Ow!" the girl cried. "Did you see that?"

"We sure did," the other girls said. Soon they were pushing and hitting Gracie and Mary Kate.

Emily didn't have much experience fighting, but she wasn't going to let her friends be hurt. She stood up and rammed the first girl against a tree, then began kicking her. One of the other girls pulled her off, and she swung wildly at her. She was pushed down onto the road again and again, and each time she got up kicking and swinging.

"Girls, stop this immediately!"

"Now we're in trouble," Mary Kate said.

Emily stood up and tried to brush the dirt off her uniform. Gracie was standing next to her, wiping her nose and eyes. Mary Kate was a few feet away, surrounded by the bullying girls. Everyone was dirty, and Emily could see cuts and bruises on just about all of them.

"We're sorry, Miss Upshaw," the girl in the middy said. "We were walking to school, minding our own business, and the girls from the Home wouldn't let us get past them. They never care if they're late to school, and we said excuse me, but they just laughed, and then this new girl, the one without any hair, she pushed poor Florrie, and I admit it, I got so angry, I pushed her right back. I guess it's all my fault. I'll take any punishment you think is right."

"That's just what happened," the third girl said. "She picked on Florrie."

"I did not," Emily said. "That isn't what happened at all."

"I wouldn't have minded if she'd picked on me," the girl in the middy said. "But pushing poor Florrie that way. It just made me so angry."

"Florrie, is Harriet telling the truth?" Miss Upshaw asked.

As the second girl walked toward Miss Upshaw, Emily could see she had a pronounced limp. "That's just what happened," she said. "I know I walk slower than other girls, but I don't think it was right of her to push me like that. Please forgive Harriet. She's always trying to defend me from the orphan home girls."

"My mother says it's a crime that we have to go to school with girls from the Home," the third girl said. "She says they come from the dregs of society."

"They're lying," Emily said. "Mary Kate and Gracie and I were walking to school, minding our own business, and these girls came and insulted us and that big one over there pushed me onto the ground. And I do not come from the dregs of society."

The town girls tittered.

"I don't," Emily insisted. "My mother was a Lathrop. The Lathrop name stands for something."

"I bet your father doesn't have a name," the third girl whispered so softly only Emily could hear her.

"Stop that!" Emily cried, and gave the girl a shove. The girl promptly burst into tears.

"Very well, I've seen enough," Miss Upshaw said. She grabbed Emily by the ear and pulled her away. "The rest of you girls, go to school immediately. I'll deal with the other girls from the orphan home later."

"But it's not my fault," Emily said.

"Quiet!" Miss Upshaw said. She released her grasp on Emily's ear, grabbing her by her arm instead, and pulling her toward the schoolhouse. "You orphan girls are the worst," she declared. "Guttersnipes one and all. But attacking a poor cripple girl. That's truly despicable."

"But I didn't," Emily said.

"I told you to keep quiet," Miss Upshaw said.

Emily's arm ached, her ear hurt, and she could feel bruises on her knee and her side from being pushed. She only hoped Harriet and the other girls hurt as much as she did.

Miss Upshaw marched Emily up the stairs. Everybody was looking at them, and Emily felt her face turn bright red. Her hair was so short, she was sure her scalp was blushing as well. She would have preferred being damned for all eternity than to be where she was at that moment.

"I don't even know your name," Miss Upshaw said when they reached her office.

"I'm Emily Lathrop Hasbrouck," Emily said.

"And this is your first day here?" Miss Upshaw asked.

Emily nodded.

"Speak when you're addressed!" Miss Upshaw said.

"Yes, ma'am," Emily said. "I'm sorry. This is my first day here."

"And you viciously attacked a cripple girl," Miss Upshaw said. "That's how you thought to begin your time with us?"

"I didn't attack her," Emily said. "The other girls started it. They were making fun of us and they pushed me."

"The girls you're accusing come from some of the finest families in this town," Miss Upshaw said. "Harriet Dale's father is the mayor of Oakbridge. Florrie Sheldon's father owns the mill. Isabella Cosgrove's father is a judge. And these are the girls you've accused of pushing you?"

"They did push me," Emily said. "It wasn't my fault, and it certainly wasn't Mary Kate's or Gracie's. They were defending me. The other girls started it, and they're the ones who should be punished. And I come from a fine family, too. My mother was a Lathrop. My aunt Mabel was a pillar of the community. You can ask anybody in Madison."

"Madison is sixty miles away," Miss Upshaw said. "Who you were in Madison, who your family was, does not pertain. You are an Austen girl now, and like many of the girls there, you are little better than trash. A girl who attacks a cripple is not fit for social intercourse."

"But I didn't attack her," Emily said. "Why won't you believe me?"

"I know Florrie, Harriet, and Isabella," Miss Upshaw said. "I go to church with them and their families. They are all upstanding members of this community, and it is natural I should take their word over yours. I am going to telephone Miss Browne now and tell her exactly what happened today, and urge her to punish you until you are truly repentant for your deed."

Emily knew she was never going to be repentant, but years of living with Aunt Mabel had taught her the wisdom of keeping her mouth shut. She continued to stand as Miss Upshaw left her office to use the telephone, and she maintained her silence even as the matron from the orphan home came to take her back while everybody in the playground stared at her and laughed.

Chapter 4

"It doesn't matter who started it," Miss Browne told Emily. "It doesn't matter that Harriet Dale pushed you. It doesn't matter that your mother was a Lathrop. The only thing that matters is that you're an Austen girl, and the Austen Home is dependent on the charity of the people of Oakbridge."

Emily looked down at the floor. It still mattered to her, no matter what Miss Browne said.

"Harriet Dale's father and Isabella Cosgrove's father are both on the board of trustees of the Austen Home," Miss Browne said. "Florrie Sheldon's father donates the material for your uniforms. Without that material, we'd have to get our clothing from the church poor boxes. Would you prefer that?"

Emily shook her head.

"The people of Oakbridge have very mixed feelings about this home," Miss Browne said. "They're good charitable people, and they want to help out. But we cost them a great deal of money and we give them very little in return. They don't want to have to think about us. They'll send their children to school with ours just as long as the Austen girls know their place. And their place does not include pushing and fighting."

"What was I supposed to do?" Emily asked.

Miss Browne sighed. "You were supposed to ignore them," she said. "I know the Austen girls get teased. I know you're called hogs, and other words I could never repeat. I wish it weren't that way, but it is. And your response should be simple acceptance. Turn the other cheek."

"Then I don't want to be an Austen girl," Emily said.

"Nobody wants to be an Austen girl," Miss Browne said. "Nobody chooses to live in an orphan asylum. But you have no other family willing to take care of you, and believe me, this home is a thousand times better than a city asylum or the streets. In a year or two, if everyone has forgotten this unfortunate incident, we'll try to find employment for you. Perhaps Mr. Sheldon will let you work at his mill."

Had it only been a week ago that Emily lived with her aunt Mabel? And now she was being promised a life as a maid or a mill worker. Emily swallowed her tears.

"You must be punished," Miss Browne said. "But not harshly. Not this time. I'm going to send you back to the isolation room. You'll stay there until breakfast tomorrow morning. In the meantime, you'll fast and repent, and use the time to think about what it means to be an Austen girl. I'll expect you to write letters of apology to Harriet, Florrie, and Isabella. And one to Miss Upshaw too, since you were undoubtedly rude to her."

"Don't punish Mary Kate or Gracie," Emily said. "They were just defending me."

"They should have known better than to fight with the town girls," Miss Browne said. "They'll go without supper tonight, and write letters of apology as well. You are now dismissed."

Emily followed Matron up the stairs and listened as Matron slammed the door behind her and locked it. Emily knew she was getting off fairly lightly. Aunt Mabel had been a firm believer in spare the rod and spoil the child, and Emily had always felt fortunate when her punishment was banishment to her room with no supper. It was the injustice that galled her, not the hunger and loneliness she knew she'd be feeling.

The isolation room had a window that overlooked the orphan home's play area. Emily stood by the window and stared hard into her future. She didn't like any of the possibilities she could imagine. Mill worker. Domestic. Four more years at the orphan home. Four years of taking whatever

39

Harriet Dale, Florrie Sheldon, and Isabella Cosgrove had to offer, with no way of fighting back.

Emily tried telling herself that things would get better. Her hair would grow back, after all, and she had already made friends. Soon there'd be another new girl at the home for Harriet and her friends to pick on. She liked the idea of going to school. A town the size of Oakbridge might have a piano in its school, and possibly there were no rules forbidding the Austen girls to use it. Emily could hear Aunt Mabel telling her her trials were God's way of punishing her for her innumerable sins. She should pray for forgiveness, and learn to be grateful for the many blessings He had bestowed upon her.

In spite of herself, Emily thought about her sister. It didn't matter that she didn't know where her sister lived, or even what her name was. They were kin, and kin belonged together. Emily was positive that if she were allowed to live with her sister and her family, she'd be just as good as Aunt Mabel and Reverend Dowling wanted her to be. She'd be quiet and respectful, and play the piano just beautifully. God certainly wouldn't punish her for leaving the Austen Home and finding her way to her sister.

The next morning, apologies in hand, Emily walked to school with Mary Kate and Gracie. "When are you planning to run away?" she asked Mary Kate.

"I have to wait until I have bosoms," Mary Kate said.

"Mary Kate!" Gracie said, but then she giggled.

"All actresses have bosoms," Mary Kate said. "Rich men only like girls who have them."

"When do you think you'll be getting them?" Emily asked.

"I don't know," Mary Kate said. "Maybe in a couple of years."

"Martha Smith has enormous bosoms," Gracie said. "But she's fifteen."

"Her name is Smith too?" Emily asked.

"All the foundlings are named Smith," Gracie said. "Except the ones that come with names. Bertha Downing is a foundling, but the note with her said her name was Downing so she isn't a Smith."

"Downing probably wasn't her real name," Mary Kate said. "They looked all over for a family named Downing that could have had a baby, and there weren't any."

"Maybe it was her father's name," Gracie said. "Anyway, she isn't a Smith. She has bosoms, though. Not as big as Martha Smith's, but she has them."

"Are you thinking about running away?" Mary Kate asked.

Emily nodded. "But I don't think I can wait until you get bosoms," she said.

"What would you do?" Gracie asked. "Where would you live?"

"With my sister," Emily said. "We're kin. It's only right we should be together."

"But doesn't she have parents of her own?" Gracie asked.

"If they took her in, they'll take me in too," Emily said. "Good Christian people like that. It's what my sister would want, and they want her to be happy. I'll go live with them, and go all the way through high school, and lead a respectable Christian life."

"That sounds wonderful," Gracie said. "Almost as good as living with your mother, the way I'm going to."

"I thought you didn't know where your sister lived," Mary Kate said.

"I don't," Emily said. "But I was thinking about how you read the note that came with you. The one you found in Miss Browne's files. I bet she has papers about me in there, and those papers say where my sister is."

"Do you think she'll show them to you?" Gracie asked. "If you ask her nice? Miss Browne is always saying how she wants what's best for us Austen girls. I bet she thinks you should live with your sister. That would certainly be what's best for you."

"She isn't going to show Emily anything," Mary Kate said. "They never want you to know about your family. Has Miss Browne ever shown you anything about your mother?"

Gracie shook her head. "But maybe it'd be different with Emily," she said. "Maybe Miss Browne isn't used to having her around yet."

"Emily's going to have to sneak into Miss Browne's office, the way I did," Mary Kate said.

"Then I'm doing it tonight," Emily said. "I don't want to stay here any longer than I have to. My sister's waited her whole life for me to live with her. It isn't fair for me to keep her waiting any longer."

"When you find out where she is, what'll you do?" Gracie asked. "How will you get there?"

"I don't know yet," Emily said. "First things first. Tonight, when it's real late, I'll sneak down there and read my file."

"I'll miss you," Gracie said. "I know I don't know you very well, and because of you I got into trouble, but I like you anyway, Emily. You make things interesting."

"I'll miss you too," Emily said. "Both of you. But I owe it to my mother to find my sister and be with her. That's what she must have wanted for us."

"And it gets you out of here," Mary Kate said.

"That too," Emily said, and they all laughed.

"Look at this! It's the hogs, and this time they're laughing."

Emily turned to her right and saw Harriet Dale and her friends approaching them.

"So they're letting you into our school," Harriet said. "Even after you attacked poor Florrie."

Emily clutched her letters of apology. She wished she could ram them down Harriet's throat.

"We didn't have nearly enough time yesterday to say what we thought about you hogs," Harriet said. "Of course, we should have expected you to attack us the way you did. Animals like you belong in hog pens, not in schools with decent people."

"My father says if you come anywhere near me he'll see to it that you go to jail," Florrie said. "He already spoke to Judge Cosgrove about you, and Judge Cosgrove said any girl who would knock over a poor cripple should be locked up for life."

Emily didn't remember knocking Florrie over. Then again, she didn't remember not knocking her over either. "I'm sorry if I knocked you over," she said, just to be on the safe side.

"Listen to that!" Harriet said. "The hog is apologizing. I guess she doesn't want to go to jail."

"Jail's even worse than the orphan asylum," Isabella said. "At least when you get old enough, they kick you out of the asylum. Jail you have to stay in forever."

"I don't know," Harriet said. "Garbage is garbage. I bet most of the hogs end up in jail anyway."

"If they don't they should," Florrie declared. "My mother said she's tried to have girls from the asylum work for us as servants, but they can never be trusted. She says every time she's tried to teach one of them how to work, the girl has talked back or stolen something and she's had to fire her without references. You know what becomes of servants without references."

"They end up on the streets," Isabella said. "With all the other hogs."

"I don't think this hog will do too well on the streets," Harriet said. "Men prefer hogs with hair."

The girls all laughed. In spite of herself, Emily touched her short-cropped head.

"I bet this hog was full of lice," Harriet said.

"Not just lice," Isabella said. "All kinds of bugs. Disgusting."

"It isn't right we should have to be in the same school with them," Florrie said. "My mother says I should be going to a private school with only the best girls."

"Why don't you then?" Isabella asked.

"My father won't pay for it," Florrie said. "My brothers go to a military academy, but Father says public school is good enough for me. He says I shouldn't have expectations."

"That's terrible," Emily said.

"What did you say?" Florrie asked. "Were you talking to me, you filthy hog?"

"I'm sorry," Emily said.

"She was insulting me and my father," Florrie said. "An animal like that."

"I guess she hasn't learned her lesson yet," Harriet said. She grabbed Emily by her shoulders. "Hogs don't speak to humans," she said. "Say that."

"Hogs don't speak to humans," Emily muttered.

"Say it louder!"

"Hogs don't speak to humans," Emily said. She could see Mary Kate and Gracie standing by her side and willed them to keep out of it. It was bad enough what was happening to her. They shouldn't have to get into more trouble.

"Hogs shouldn't walk on the same sidewalks as humans," Isabella said. "Look how upset poor Florrie is just having to be near this ugly bald hog."

"You're right, Isabella," Harriet said. "That's what I was trying to teach this hog yesterday. She needs to learn some manners."

"She needs to learn her place," Florrie said.

Emily felt Harriet's grip on her shoulders grow stronger. "I'm sorry," she said. "I'll learn my place, honest."

Harriet laughed. "Hear that, girls," she said. "The hog wants to learn her place."

"Teach it to her," Florrie said. "Teach it to her right now."

"I guess I'd better," Harriet said. She gave Emily a hard push onto the ground. "That's your place, hog," she said. "In the gutter."

"Harriet Dale, what are you doing?"

Emily looked up, expecting to find Miss Upshaw. But instead she saw a much younger woman, and one who didn't seem to be angry at her.

"She tripped, Miss Webber," Harriet said. "See, I was just helping her up."

"You pushed her," Miss Webber said. "I saw you push her, Harriet, and I heard some of the terrible things you called her."

"That's because she was going to push Florrie," Harriet said. "A poor cripple like that."

"She was nowhere near Florrie," Miss Webber said. "And even if she had been, you had a stranglehold on her. Here, child, let me help you up." She reached a hand down for Emily, who took it gratefully.

"You'd better watch what you say to me," Harriet said. "Are you accusing me of being a liar?"

"I'm not accusing you of anything," Miss Webber said. "What you are is between the Good Lord and yourself to work out."

"My father's the mayor, you know," Harriet said. "He could get you fired."

"No, he can't," Miss Webber said. "The mayor is not responsible for the librarian. I know you think your father is a very important man, but believe me, Harriet, he is not in charge of the universe. Now, why don't you go to school and use your energy on self-improvement?"

"It isn't fair," Harriet said, but she and her friends walked away from Emily, Mary Kate, and Gracie.

"Thank you," Emily said.

"You're very welcome," Miss Webber said. "My name is Alice Webber, and as you may have gathered, I'm the town librarian. I don't believe I know any of you girls."

"I'm Emily Hasbrouck," Emily said. "And these are my friends, Gracie Dodge and Mary Kate Smith."

"I don't see enough of you Austen girls in the library," Miss Webber said. "You have permission to go after school, you know. Miss Browne and I have discussed it, and we both think it would be a great benefit to you if you used the library more."

"I'd go," Gracie said. "But my chores have to be done after school. And Mary Kate here doesn't like to read."

"What about you, Emily?" Miss Webber asked. "Do you like to read?"

"Yes, ma'am," Emily said. "I used to read a lot."

"Then I hope I'll be seeing you at the library," Miss Webber said. "Do you know where it is?"

Emily shook her head. "No, ma'am," she said.

"It's two blocks down from the school building," Miss Webber told her. "And I'm sure we have many books you'd enjoy reading. I hope I'll see you there soon. As a matter of fact, why don't I walk you to your school today, and I can point out to you just where the library is as we go."

"Thank you, ma'am," Emily said. She knew Miss Webber was offering her and her friends protection until they got to the school, and she was grateful for it. She liked the idea of going to the library as well, and finding books to read. But no matter how much of a sanctuary the library might be, Emily had no intention of becoming attached to it. Not when she had a sister and a home of her own to get to.

✦ Chapter 5

Emily had spent much of the past four years tip-
toeing around her aunt Mabel's house. Now that
she thought about it, she'd tiptoed a fair amount
when her father had fallen asleep at the kitchen
table. She was accustomed to moving silently. She
only hoped Mary Kate was as practiced as she
was.

"Don't worry," Mary Kate whispered to her as
they tiptoed down the staircase from their dormitory to Miss Browne's first-floor office. "I know
just where to look."

Emily had tried to persuade Mary Kate not to
accompany her, but Mary Kate had insisted. "You
don't know this place like I do," Mary Kate had
pointed out. "I know which stairs squeak."

"She does," Gracie had agreed. "Mary Kate

goes into the kitchen lots of times to steal food in the middle of the night."

Emily certainly didn't know which stairs squeaked, and it was a help having someone along who knew which corridors to check and which to scoot past. Thus far Mary Kate had proved an excellent guide, and it was a comfort not being alone in such a strange dark building. Emily only hoped they wouldn't get caught. It had been hard enough when she'd been punished for something that wasn't her fault. The idea that Gracie and Mary Kate had also gone without supper just for defending her was truly upsetting.

"Down here," Mary Kate whispered, as they safely made it to the front hallway. "This way."

Emily held on to Mary Kate's hand and followed her to Miss Browne's office door. Mary Kate bent down and looked under the crack in the doorway.

"No light on," she whispered. "We're safe." She opened the door very slowly, and she and Emily slipped into the office.

"I can't see anything," Emily whispered.

"Turn the light on," Mary Kate said. "I'll keep an eye out in the hallway to make sure no one is coming."

Emily felt her way around the room until she located Miss Browne's desk. She could feel a lamp there. It was electric, and Emily had never turned on an electric light before. Aunt Mabel didn't approve of electric. Emily fumbled about, until she discovered that if she tightened the glass inside the lamp, light magically appeared.

In spite of herself, Emily laughed with delight.

"Shush!" Mary Kate whispered.

"Sorry," Emily whispered back.

"The files are alphabetical," Mary Kate said. "Look under H."

Emily almost pointed out that she knew just where in the alphabet she was going to find Hasbrouck, but this wasn't the moment to quarrel. She pictured Mary Kate looking for her file under Smith, and wondered how many Smiths she'd had to go through before finding the right one.

Luckily, she was the only Hasbrouck. She pulled out the file and took it to the desk to read.

It was a thin file and didn't take long to go through. There was a report from the nurse who had examined her that indicated Emily was perfectly healthy. There was a birth certificate for Emily and death certificates for Emily's parents and Aunt Mabel. There was a letter from Aunt Mabel's lawyer saying that Emily's mother was a Lathrop who had married beneath her and died in childbirth when Emily was three; that her father was a penniless drunkard who died when a train hit him and was believed to be a suicide; and that her aunt Mabel's entire estate had been left to the First Methodist Church of Madison to be used for missionary work in Africa. And there was a form, labeled HASBROUCK, EMILY LATHROP, that listed Emily's birth date, height, weight, hair and eye color, family status (orphaned), church affiliation, and grade level. In the space for additional comments was one note:

Emily has a younger sister who was given away for adoption at the time of her mother's death. Emily seems unduly interested in this sister, and has not yet accepted her own lot in life.

And that was it. Emily looked through the file again, hoping to find some slip of paper that she had missed, but there was nothing. No name, no address, nothing but some nasty words about her father and a snide comment about her undue interest in the only family member she had left.

"Anything?" Mary Kate whispered.

Emily shook her head.

"You'd better put it back then," Mary Kate said.

Emily did as she was told. She hated them all, she thought, as she carefully put the file back where she'd found it. She hated Aunt Mabel and Aunt Mabel's lawyer and Miss Browne. She even hated her father for agreeing to give his baby daughter up for adoption.

"Turn the light out," Mary Kate whispered, as though Emily wouldn't have known to. The glass burned Emily's fingers as she loosened it until the light went off. Emily rubbed her fingers angrily and followed Mary Kate out of the room and back against the hallway walls, up the stairs, carefully avoiding the ones that creaked, and, most dangerously, back into the dormitory, under the snoring nose of the matron.

Mary Kate fell asleep almost instantly, but Emily spent most of the night awake. She couldn't remember the last night she'd slept well, the last night she hadn't had a thousand things to worry about or be miserable over. Before Aunt Mabel got sick, she decided. Before she'd really understood she was an orphan and what an orphan's lot truly was.

Emily dreaded getting up the next morning, hated sharing the lavatory with twenty other girls, hated setting places for forty at breakfast, and then hated even more clearing their plates and piling them up in the sink for others to wash. She hardly spoke to Mary Kate or Gracie as the three of them walked to school together.

"Look at this. It's the hogs again!"

"Just keep walking," Mary Kate whispered.

"I never knew hogs could be so ugly," Isabella said. "Look at their dirty ugly dresses."

"The bald one's the ugliest," Harriet said. "She's stupid, too. Miss Upshaw told my mother she didn't even go to school back in her old hog pen."

"My father says if she says one more mean thing to me, I should tell him and he'll never give another thing to the orphan asylum again," Florrie declared. "He said it's wrong to give charity to the less fortunate if they're not meek and humble enough to appreciate it."

"I think she should go to jail," Harriet said. "I bet she's done all kinds of bad things like stealing. The way she pushed you around, Florrie, well, it just proves what an evil hog she is."

Emily, Mary Kate, and Gracie kept on walking. The other girls followed them, and sure enough, Harriet gave Emily a push. Emily fell facedown onto the sidewalk. She could feel the concrete scrape the skin off her nose.

Before Emily had a chance to get up, Isabella gave her a kick on her side. Then she, Harriet, and Florrie walked away from them, laughing as they went.

Mary Kate and Gracie helped Emily get up. As they did, Miss Webber ran over to them.

"I'm too late, I see," Miss Webber said as she joined them. "Was it the same girls as yesterday?"

"It doesn't matter," Emily said. "I'm all right."

"Your nose is bleeding," Miss Webber said. "Go to the school nurse right away so she can clean and bandage it."

Emily touched her nose, and found a little bit of blood on her finger. "It isn't bad," she said, although her face and side were both throbbing.

"I'm going to telephone all those girls' parents tonight," Miss Webber said. "In fact, I'll walk with you to school and tell Miss Upshaw about them as well."

"No, don't do that," Emily said. "Please don't tell anybody."

"Why not?" Miss Webber said. "Those girls have to be stopped."

"Really," Mary Kate said. "It's okay."

"They don't mean any harm," Gracie said. "They're just having fun."

"It isn't fun pushing another girl," Miss Webber said. "It's bullying and it's wrong and they should be punished."

"No," Emily said. "It doesn't matter what they did."

Miss Webber sighed. "I'm going to take you to the nurse's office," she said. "And I'm going to tell Miss Upshaw what I saw. I'm sorry, girls, but I have an obligation to do that."

"They won't get in trouble," Emily said. "We will."

"She's right," Mary Kate said. "We'll be blamed."

"Not after I explain to Miss Upshaw just what I witnessed," Miss Webber said.

"They'll just lie," Emily said. "They'll tell her I fell and they were just helping me up. They'll try to get you in trouble, and they'll make things worse for us too."

"Miss Browne says we have to turn the other cheek," Gracie said.

"And if we don't, we'll just get punished even more," Mary Kate said.

"This makes me so angry," Miss Webber said. "It's wrong the way those girls are treating you."

"Then they'll go to Hell," Gracie said. "And we'll go to Heaven."

"Small comfort," Miss Webber said. "At least in this lifetime. I'll tell you what. I'll take Emily to the nurse's office, and then when I get to the library, I'll telephone Miss Browne and discuss the situation with her. That won't get you in any more trouble, and maybe the two of us can work something out."

"Thank you," Emily said, because Aunt Mabel had taught her to be polite.

"Thank you," the other girls said.

They walked the remaining distance to the school in silence. Miss Webber escorted Emily to the nurse's office and watched as the nurse cleaned Emily's wounds.

"Come to the library after school," Miss Webber said. "We'll talk there."

Emily nodded. She hated the thought of going into her classroom and seeing Harriet, Florrie, and Isabella sitting there, laughing at her, but she had no choice. At least she hadn't been summoned to Miss Upshaw's office for further punishment.

The school day went by slowly and it was hard for Emily to concentrate on what the teacher was saying. At lunch, all the Austen girls sat by themselves at two tables in the back, while the other boys and girls used the rest of the lunchroom. Emily saw some of them pointing at her and laughing.

She knew she must make quite a sight. Her uniform was filthy from three days of being pushed onto the sidewalk, she had a bandage on her nose and a bruise on her cheek, and her hair hadn't even begun growing back.

At the end of the school day, Emily watched as Mary Kate and Gracie joined some of the Austen girls on the walk back to the Home. She went in the other direction to the library. She doubted Miss Webber had come up with any way of keeping Harriet and the others from plaguing her, but she appreciated the effort the librarian wanted to make.

"I'm glad you came," Miss Webber said when Emily walked in. "Come into my office, and we'll chat."

Emily nodded. The library was a large, well-lit room, filled with shelves and shelves of books. She'd forgotten how much she'd enjoyed reading.

"May I take a book out?" she asked. "I promise I'll return it right away."

"Of course you may," Miss Webber said. "We'll make a library card up for you, and you'll be able to take two books out at a time whenever you want."

"Thank you," Emily said. "I'd like that."

Miss Webber smiled at her. "First, let's have our little chat," she said. "And then you can look at every book we have and decide which ones you want to take out today."

Emily followed Miss Webber into her office. It

was a small room, much smaller than Miss Browne's office, and its window overlooked the main street in Oakbridge. Emily watched as buggies and wagons rode by, and even saw a few automobiles drive past them.

"Soon everyone will be driving automobiles," Miss Webber said. "I own one, you know."

"You do?" Emily asked.

"It's my pride and joy," Miss Webber said. "When the road is good, I can drive twenty-five miles an hour."

"But isn't that dangerous?" Emily asked.

"I'm very careful," Miss Webber replied. "All good drivers are. Would you like me to take you for a ride one day?"

"Oh, yes," Emily said. "That would be so exciting."

"We will, then," Miss Webber said. "It'll be fun."

Miss Webber sat on the edge of her desk and beckoned for Emily to sit in the chair facing her. Emily had never seen a woman sit like that before, perched on a piece of furniture, but Miss Webber seemed comfortable enough, and it was her office.

"I did what I told you I was going to do and nothing more," Miss Webber said. "I telephoned Miss Browne and discussed your situation with her."

"Yes," Emily said.

Miss Webber frowned. "She reacted much the way you and your friends said she would," she admitted. "She said the Austen Home was very dependent on the Dales and the Sheldons and the Cosgroves and the other prominent families in Oakbridge and that she couldn't do anything that might anger or provoke them. She also said there had been other incidents in the past, and that the policy of the board of trustees of the Austen Home was to accept any blame that the community assigned them for the misbehavior of the Austen girls and punish them accordingly."

"Whether we're guilty or not," Emily said.

"I'm afraid so," Miss Webber said. "I pointed out to her that that was wrong, both for the Austen girls, and also for the children who tormented them, who would then feel that they could get away with that sort of behavior free of punishment. Miss Browne said it couldn't be helped and that someday the meek would inherit the earth and things would even out."

"She said that?" Emily asked.

"And more," Miss Webber said. "But I'd best not repeat all of it to you. We had quite a talk."

"But it doesn't matter," Emily said. "Not until the meek inherit the earth, I mean. Harriet and her friends can keep on doing whatever they want to me, and I have to accept it."

"I'm still willing to speak to their parents," Miss Webber said. "Or to Miss Upshaw. The Dales and the Sheldons don't own me."

Emily shook her head. "Please don't bother," she said. "It will only make things worse."

"You may be right," Miss Webber said. "It makes me so angry. One day soon women will have the vote, and the instant that happens, I'm going to run for mayor myself. How I'd love to boot William Dale out of office."

"My aunt Mabel didn't think women should vote," Emily said.

"Your aunt Mabel was wrong," Miss Webber replied.

Emily was shocked. No one had ever suggested to her before that Aunt Mabel could be wrong about anything. Emily found she rather liked that idea.

"Nothing against your aunt Mabel," Miss Webber said. "I'm sure she was a very fine woman."

"She was," Emily said. "She took me in and raised me after my father died."

"That was good of her," Miss Webber said. "I'm sure you must miss her a great deal."

Emily began to cry.

"Oh, dear, I'm sorry," Miss Webber said. "Here, take my handkerchief. Oh, I didn't mean to upset you. Of course you miss your aunt. How thoughtless of me to say all those things about her."

Emily took the handkerchief and mopped the tears off her cheek. It hurt to even touch the bruise, and she had to force herself not to cry out in pain. "I don't miss her," she said. "Not really. I just hate it here so much."

"I don't blame you," Miss Webber said. "Although Miss Browne means well. She really does."

"I have a family," Emily said. "A real family. I have a sister."

"You do?" Miss Webber asked.

Emily blew her nose and nodded. "She's younger than me, but she's my sister," she said. "My father gave her to people to raise when our mother died. And all I want is to find my sister and nobody will help me."

"I will," Miss Webber said. "You tell me everything you know about your sister, and we'll find her together."

"I don't know anything," Emily wailed. "I don't even know her name."

"Oh, my," Miss Webber said. "That will certainly make things harder."

"She's lost forever," Emily said. "I'm sure she worries about me, the same as I worry about her. And I know my mother would want us to be together."

"I'll tell you what," Miss Webber said. "You fill out a library card, and take out a book or two, and by the time you return them, I'll have figured out a way we can find your sister."

"Will you really?" Emily asked.

"I certainly will," Miss Webber said. "If you have a family, the best thing for you and for the Austen Home would be if you could go live with them forever."

✛ Chapter 6

The next morning before breakfast, Emily, Gracie, and Mary Kate were called into Miss Browne's office.

"I know you girls have had a hard time of it this week," Miss Browne told them. "Sometimes the town children can be quite cruel."

Emily and her friends stood there silently. At least they weren't about to be punished, Emily thought.

"I've come up with a temporary solution," Miss Browne said. "For the next few days at least, I want you three girls to leave for school fifteen minutes early. And when you get to school, you are to go in immediately and take your seats. That way you'll avoid seeing the girls who have been tormenting you."

"Thank you, Miss Browne," Gracie said, and Mary Kate also said thanks.

"I can't leave for school early," Emily said. "I clear the breakfast dishes."

"I'd forgotten that," Miss Browne said. "Very well. You'll go by yourself, Emily, at least until we can find a different chore for you to do. Gracie, Mary Kate, you're dismissed. Emily, please stay here for another minute."

Emily watched as her friends left. She was happy for them that they wouldn't be stuck protecting her, relieved for herself that she wouldn't be responsible for what happened to them anymore, and absolutely miserable at the thought that she'd have to confront Harriet and the others on her own.

"I had two conversations with Alice Webber yesterday," Miss Browne said. "In the morning she called because she was concerned about what was going on, and I was grateful to hear her report. Then late yesterday afternoon, she called again, to discuss you just a little bit."

"Yes, ma'am," Emily said. Had Miss Webber told Miss Browne about Emily's plan to find her sister? Emily knew she'd be in trouble if she had.

"Miss Webber asked me if you might have supper with her and her mother this evening," Miss Browne said. "She said you'd gone to the library after school yesterday, and she'd enjoyed talking with you, and thought her mother might like to meet you as well. I told her I'd ask you and if you wanted, it was fine with me."

"Really?" Emily asked.

Miss Browne smiled. "I know you must think I'm some sort of ogre," she said. "And I grant you, we haven't gotten off to the best of starts. But I like my girls to be happy, and I think it's good for them to have contact with real families and make friends outside of the Austen Home. I've known the Webbers for years, and there are no finer women in this town. Any friendship that might develop could only be beneficial to you. Would you like to join them for supper tonight?"

"Oh, yes," Emily said.

"Very well," Miss Browne said. "I'll telephone Miss Webber at the library and tell her to expect you after school today. She'll bring you back here after supper. Perhaps if it isn't too late, she'll take you back in her automobile. I've ridden in it myself, and it's quite an experience."

"Thank you," Emily said.

"Remember, Emily, the first week at Austen is always the hardest," Miss Browne said. "It does get easier as time goes by. And please, Emily, if you do run into Harriet Dale and the others this morning, practice Christian forbearance and remember no matter how they may try to hurt you, they're hurting themselves far more."

"Yes, ma'am," Emily said. She left the office and went straight to the dining room and began setting the tables for breakfast.

Emily left the Home as early as she could and made a point of running to the school in an effort to get there before Harriet and the others. The other Austen girls were avoiding her, and she couldn't blame them, but she felt lonely and vulnerable.

"It's the hog!"

"Here, piggy, piggy, piggy."

"That's hoggy, hoggy, hoggy."

Emily blushed but kept on walking. Maybe they'd be satisfied just calling her names. She could deal with that. Aunt Mabel had on more than one occasion called her a no-account Hasbrouck or made dire predictions about how she was doomed to be like her drunken father. "Hog" was nothing compared to that.

"What's the matter, hog? Are you deaf or something?"

"Hogs are animals. Animals don't know English."

"My father says hogs shouldn't be allowed in our school. He says there's no need for them to have any kind of education, since all they're going to do is be our servants or work in our mills."

"That's not true. A lot of them end up in jail!"

"Get off the sidewalk, hog. Animals should be on the street, not where decent people walk."

Emily swallowed hard. She wanted to stand her ground. She had as much right to be on the sidewalk as any of them. Even if she hadn't been half Lathrop, she had a right to the sidewalk. But she didn't dare provoke a fight, and she was tired of being pushed onto the ground. So she stepped off the sidewalk and onto the street.

"That's better. At least now the hogs are learning their place."

Emily's humiliation seemed to be enough for Harriet and the others that day. They made oinking sounds as they passed Emily, and she noted that they kept turning around and staring at her to make sure she hadn't gotten back onto the sidewalk, but at least they hadn't physically attacked her. She made it to the schoolhouse with her uniform, if not her dignity, intact, went to her seat immediately, and ignored all the other children as they came in.

She could hardly wait for the school day to end. Naturally, it felt like forever before the final bell rang and the children were released. Emily said good-bye to Gracie and Mary Kate and went directly to the library.

"Hello, Emily," Miss Webber said. "I'm glad you're joining us. Have you had a chance to read the book you took out yet?"

"I thought I'd read it here," Emily said. "It gets noisy at the Home. It's hard to find a quiet place to read."

"That's what libraries are for," Miss Webber said. "I think of them as sanctuaries from the noise of the world. Why don't you sit at that table, and if anybody gets talkative, I'll be sure to shush them."

Emily smiled her gratitude to Miss Webber

and took a seat at the table. She opened the book, and soon she found herself immersed in the story. It was a pleasure to read about somebody else's problems for a change.

At five P.M. Miss Webber began closing up the library. Emily offered to help, and Miss Webber gave her a couple of simple jobs to do. Once the librarian was satisfied that the library was ready for closing, she ushered Emily out, then locked the door. As they walked the five blocks to her home, Miss Webber pointed out various sights to Emily.

Emily had hardly had a chance to see Oakridge in the week or so since she'd moved to the orphan home. She was surprised to discover what a pretty town it was, and how big and busy. Miss Webber said hello to many people as they walked, including several children who were outside playing. The children stared at Emily, but at least none of them insulted her. Emily liked being with Miss Webber. It made her feel important to be with such an important person. She also liked seeing how up-to-date Oakbridge was. She counted six automobiles driving at terrifying speeds in just the five blocks. There were poles for telephones and electricity. It was too early for the streetlights to be on, but Miss Webber told her they were electric also. Aunt Mabel certainly wouldn't have approved of Oakbridge.

Miss Webber's house was white with green shutters and it had a wraparound porch. Parked in front of the house was her automobile. "Would you like to sit inside it?" she asked.

"May I?" Emily asked. "I've never been in an automobile."

"I'll drive you home tonight," Miss Webber said. "But we can sit in it now, too, if you'd like."

Emily raced to the automobile. Miss Webber told her to open the door and climb in, so she did. The seat was firm, almost hard, but it was at least as comfortable as a buggy and it felt a lot more exciting.

"Maybe someday I'll teach you how to drive," Miss Webber said. "I'm teaching my mother now, and if I can survive that, I can survive anything."

Emily laughed. The sound of her laughter startled her, and she realized it had been months since she'd laughed.

"Let's go in now," Miss Webber said. "I work up a fierce appetite at the library."

Emily followed Miss Webber into her house. She couldn't imagine a prettier one. There were lace curtains on the windows, and landscape paintings on the walls, and lots of shelves filled with books. On the front-parlor floor was a carpet of maroon and blue and green in strange and exotic designs.

"That's a Persian carpet," Miss Webber told her. "My father brought it back from the Orient. It's my mother's prized possession."

"You have a piano," Emily said, as she spotted the upright in the corner.

"It was my father's," Miss Webber said. "He loved playing the piano. Mother and I don't play very well, but we keep it in his memory."

"I play the piano," Emily said. "My father taught me how." She couldn't believe she had told Miss Webber that. Not even Mrs. James had known. "And when I went to live with Aunt Mabel, I had lessons. Aunt Mabel said all the Lathrops are musical. I'm half Lathrop, you know."

"I wish I were musical," Miss Webber said. "Perhaps you could play the piano for us after supper."

"Oh, I'd love to," Emily said. "I can play hymns if you'd like. Or Chopin waltzes. That's what I was studying when my aunt died and I had to stop."

"The waltzes sound lovely," Miss Webber said. "I'm sure Mother would enjoy them as well."

Emily tried to conceal her excitement at the thought of playing the piano again. It must be wonderful to live in a house like this one, she thought. Just being a domestic here would be better than living at the Austen Home. Maybe if Miss Webber needed a servant, she could be hired right away. Miss Webber was so nice, Emily was sure she'd be allowed to play the piano when she'd finished all her tasks, the same as she had at Aunt Mabel's.

"I'm very good at cleaning," she told Miss Webber. "When my aunt Mabel got sick she let our servant girl go, and I did all the cleaning in the house. I can scrub floors and polish silver and do everything. Aunt Mabel was very fussy."

"I'm terrible at housework," Miss Webber said. "And so is my mother. Fortunately, Mrs. Macdonald comes in for us daily and keeps the house in order."

"Oh," Emily said, but Miss Webber didn't seem to notice how disappointed she was. Instead she called out to her mother.

"I'm in the kitchen," Mrs. Webber called back. "Come in and join me."

"Supper smells wonderful," Miss Webber said when they entered the kitchen. "Mother, I want you to meet Emily Hasbrouck. Emily, this is my mother, Bessie Webber."

"Pleased to meet you, ma'am," Emily said.

"Call me Aunt Bessie, child," Mrs. Webber said. "That's what children have been calling me for years."

"May I?" Emily asked.

"I won't know who you're talking to if you call me anything else," Mrs. Webber said. "Why don't you try it out? Say 'pleased to meet you, Aunt Bessie,' and if you don't like the way it sounds, you can always go back to calling me 'ma'am.' " She had a warm, easy laugh.

"Pleased to meet you, Aunt Bessie," Emily said. "I like the way that sounds."

"I do too," Aunt Bessie said. "What has this poor child been calling you, Alice?"

"Ma'am," Miss Webber said. "Or Miss Webber."

"Well, she can hardly call you Miss Webber if she's calling me Aunt Bessie," her mother said. "Why don't we try Miss Alice? We don't want you to shed too much of your dignity."

"Could I?" Emily asked.

"Miss Alice it is," the librarian said. "Emily, why don't you put your books down? Mother, are we eating in the kitchen or the dining room?"

"I thought the kitchen," Aunt Bessie said. "It seems homier to me. I thought Emily might like that."

"Yes, ma'am," Emily said. "I mean Aunt Bessie. Homier sounds wonderful to me."

"We're having nothing fancy," Aunt Bessie said. "Just shepherd's pie. I love to cook, but my work keeps me so busy, I don't have nearly enough time to."

"You work too?" Emily asked. "What do you do?"

"Mother is the telephone operator for the town," Miss Alice said. "There's nothing that goes on in Oakbridge that Mother doesn't know about."

"Not that I gossip," Aunt Bessie said. "But if you ever want to know anything about a town, speak to the town's telephone operator. We always know when the babies are born and the old folk die. Emily, why don't you help Alice set the table?

I've been trying to teach Alice how to do it proper for twenty-three years now and she's yet to learn."

"Setting tables is easy," Emily said. "I do it at the Home every morning. See, the knives go here, and the forks here. And the glasses go over here."

Miss Alice laughed. "I'm hopeless," she admitted. "Mother, I'll be out of your hair soon enough. Once Tim and I are married, you won't have to worry about how I set tables."

"Who's Tim?" Emily asked. "Oh, I'm sorry."

"What are you sorry about?" Aunt Bessie asked.

"I spoke out of turn," Emily said. "Please forgive me."

"Child, in this household you speak when you want," Aunt Bessie said. "There are no turns here. Tim is Timothy Conklin. He's Alice's intended, and they'll be married just as soon as he's finished studying to be a doctor."

"He has another year to go," Miss Alice said. "Then we'll be married."

Another year, Emily thought. When they set up their house, they'd be sure to need domestic help. She smiled at the thought. "After supper, let me wash the dishes," she said. Miss Alice might as well see now how good she was at keeping house.

"Guests don't wash dishes in this house," Aunt Bessie said. "But if you want, you can dry."

"I'm afraid not," Miss Alice said. "Emily has to get back to the Home before it gets dark."

"We'll have you over for Sunday dinner sometime, then," Aunt Bessie said. "That will give you plenty of time to dry."

"Thank you," Emily said.

"Now, let's start supper," Aunt Bessie said. "I hope you like beef barley soup, Emily, because we have plenty of it."

"I love beef barley soup," Emily said. She couldn't get over what a feast they were having. At the Home, supper was cornmeal mush with prunes for dessert.

"We have apple pie for dessert," Aunt Bessie said. "I baked it special, in your honor, Emily."

"Oh, thank you," Emily said. She felt as if she'd died and gone to Heaven.

"Alice, would you say grace?" Aunt Bessie asked, as they sat down at the table.

"Heavenly Father, we thank you for our many blessings, and ask that you look down kindly at the less fortunate, and share our bounty with them," Miss Alice said. When Aunt Bessie said "Amen," Emily joined her.

"Alice is always worrying about the less fortunate," Aunt Bessie said. "And so is Tim. The two of them aren't going to have a cent between them."

Emily's heart sank, but then she decided she'd be happy to work for them for just room and board and the chance to play the piano, and she'd swear to them she'd hardly eat at all.

"Emily, may I tell my mother about your problem?" Miss Alice asked.

"Which problem?" Emily replied.

Aunt Bessie laughed. "You poor child," she said. "How many of them do you have?"

Miss Alice smiled. "The problem about your sister," she said to Emily.

"Oh, yes," Emily said.

"It felt as if you had told me in confidence about your sister," Miss Alice said. "So I haven't discussed it with anybody."

"It was a confidence," Emily said. "But I don't mind if your mother knows."

"That's very kind of you, I'm sure," Aunt Bessie said. "Now, will you two tell me please what you're talking about? I'm near bursting with curiosity."

"Emily has a sister," Miss Alice said. "A younger sister, but she doesn't know anything about her."

"Not even her name," Emily said. "My mama died giving birth to her, and my father gave her away to a couple to raise, and I haven't seen her since."

"Emily is sure her sister wants to know where she is," Miss Alice said. "And she's hopeful that her sister's parents would want to take her in as well and give her a home."

"And you don't know anything about her?" Aunt Bessie asked. "My, that is a mystery."

"You love mysteries," Miss Alice said. "My mother's read every Sherlock Holmes story written," she said to Emily. "And she reads all the murder stories in the newspapers."

"I don't think my sister's been murdered," Emily said. "I certainly hope not."

"Not all mysteries are murders," Aunt Bessie said. "Tell me everything you know about your sister, Emily."

"I already have," Emily said. "My father never spoke about her, and neither did my aunt Mabel." She thought about admitting that she had just learned about her sister being alive, but decided not to. "I guess they thought they were protecting me, not talking about her." To Emily's surprise, she realized that they probably did think they were protecting her.

"That doesn't give us much to go on," Aunt Bessie said. "Have some bread, child. You're all skin and bones."

"You must know something more," Miss Alice said. "Your father never told you the names of the people he gave your sister to?"

"No, ma'am, I mean, Miss Alice," Emily said. "He didn't like to talk about that time. He missed my mother something fierce."

"Did you stay on in the house you were born in?" Aunt Bessie asked.

"No, Aunt Bessie," Emily said. "I don't remember the house I was born in, but my father always said it was much nicer than the house we were living in."

"Did you live in the same town?" Miss Alice asked.

Emily shook her head. "We moved a couple of

times," she said. "Papa had trouble keeping jobs after Mama died, so we had to move. Whenever we moved, he'd sell some more things, but wherever we lived, he kept the piano."

"I don't suppose you know the name of the town you were born in," Aunt Bessie said.

Emily thought about it, then realized she'd seen the name on her birth certificate. "It was Forestburg," she said. "I was born in Forestburg."

"Then the chances are your sister was born there too," Aunt Bessie said. "That's a start."

"How does that help?" Miss Alice asked.

"People have memories," Aunt Bessie replied. "Emily, do you know what church your family went to?"

"Aunt Mabel was a Methodist," Emily said. "I suppose my mother was too."

"Then tomorrow, I'll put a call in to the Methodist church in Forestburg," Aunt Bessie said, "and see if they remember what became of your baby sister."

✦ Chapter 7

Emily's trip to school the next day was relatively painless. Harriet said, "Off the sidewalk, hog," and Florrie said, "In the gutter, pig," and Isabella made a pushing gesture as she laughed, but once Emily hopped onto the street, they pretty much left her alone. It wasn't the best way to start a day, but neither was clearing off forty breakfast plates.

She managed to concentrate on school in the morning. She'd forgotten how much she'd enjoyed school. She'd learned more from Aunt Mabel, even during Aunt Mabel's illness, than she had in classes, but it was still fun to be in a classroom with other children. Not all of them were Harriet and her friends, after all. None of the town kids made any effort to befriend her, but they didn't torment her either, except for a couple of boys who called her Baldy. She could live with that.

Lunchtime was fun. At the orphan home, the girls weren't allowed to speak during meals but at the school there were no such rules, and the Austen girls made up for the enforced silences at the Home meals by chatting away continuously at the school ones. Emily liked the fact that they ate in their own corner of the room. When her hair grew out, she'd feel considerably less conspicuous, one dull blue uniform surrounded by dozens just like it.

Gracie and Mary Kate wanted to know what it had been like to have supper with the librarian and her mother, and Emily told them all about it. They nearly died when they heard she'd had apple pie for dessert.

"We have apple pies once a year," Gracie told her. "At the Fourth of July picnic. The Presbyterian church ladies bake them for us."

"We're not due for pie for another ten months," Mary Kate said. "By then I might even have bosoms."

"And you got to ride in an automobile too," Gracie said. "What was that like?"

"It was exciting but it was kind of scary," Emily replied. "We drove so fast I was sure Miss Alice, that's what I can call her, that she'd hit a dog or a cat. And we bounced a lot. Miss Alice says dirt roads aren't the best things to ride on, and someday Oakbridge will pave its roads, just like big-city streets."

"The rich men who'll buy me things will own

automobiles," Mary Kate said. "I'll ride in them all the time."

"But the best thing was the piano," Emily said. "They had a piano, and they let me play it."

"I didn't know you played the piano," Gracie said.

"I had lessons back home," Emily said. She felt a lurch of sorrow, just thinking about home. "Where I used to live, I mean. My aunt Mabel had a piano, and I used to get to play it."

"It must be wonderful not living in an orphanage," Gracie said. "Of course, I'm only in one temporarily, until my mother calls for me. But someone like Mary Kate has missed all the finer things."

"I'll stop missing them once I get bosoms," Mary Kate said.

Emily considered telling Mary Kate and Gracie about how she was going to find her sister, but decided against it. It felt odd just having told them about the piano. Aunt Mabel always said to keep private matters private, and since it had been years since Emily had had a friend, that was among the easiest of Aunt Mabel's rules to follow. And it didn't seem right sharing all her good fortune with Gracie and Mary Kate when they had so little. When Emily found her sister, and was taken in by her family, that would be the time for Gracie and Mary Kate to find out.

Just thinking about her sister made it hard for Emily to pay attention that afternoon, but it was

Friday afternoon and everybody else was restless as well. It felt as if the whole school cheered when the bell rang. Emily grabbed her things and raced over to the library.

"Have you heard anything?" she asked Miss Alice.

Miss Alice laughed. "Whatever happened to hello?" she asked.

"I'm sorry," Emily said. "Hello. Have you heard anything?"

"Not yet," Miss Alice said. "Or if Mother has, she hasn't told me."

Emily looked longingly at the telephone. Aunt Mabel hadn't had one, and Emily wasn't quite sure how to use it. That was a good thing, too, because it was all that kept her from picking it up and asking Aunt Bessie if she'd found anything out.

"Are you in a hurry to get back to the Home?" Miss Alice asked.

Miss Alice had obviously never lived in an orphan home. "No," Emily said.

"Then how about helping me out with the shelving?" Miss Alice said. "You look like a girl who knows her alphabet."

"Of course, I do," Emily said. "I can read and write. I'm not an animal."

"I'm sorry," Miss Alice said. "It was a joke, and it obviously wasn't a very good one. Would you be willing to help me out anyway?"

Emily nodded. She wasn't used to grown-ups apologizing to her. She wasn't even sure it was proper that one should. Still, it was better than a strapping for being insolent. "What do you want me to do?" she asked.

Miss Alice taught her the fundamentals of shelving, and soon Emily was busily putting books away. Miss Alice helped all the people who came into the library looking for books to read. She seemed to know all of them personally. A few of the people looked at Emily, and a couple of them whispered comments. Emily figured they weren't used to seeing Austen girls helping out in town, or maybe it was her still-dirty uniform that was bothering them. It sure bothered Emily, but laundry day wasn't until Saturday.

At four-thirty, Miss Alice told Emily to leave. Emily said good-bye to her and ran back to the orphan home, happy not to see any of her tormentors as she made her way out of town. She'd worked hard at the library, and she was sure Miss Alice had noticed how much she'd gotten done. She wanted Miss Alice to see what a good worker she was, so if there was some kind of problem about moving in with her sister, she'd still have a way out of the Austen Home.

But Emily was sure that wouldn't be necessary once she found her sister. Her sister's family were sure to want her. She was the exact same flesh and blood as her sister, so how could they not be happy to have her live with them too? And then Emily would have a mother and a father and a sister, just like Harriet and Florrie and all the other children in Oakridge.

Emily's heart raced so much at that thought she had to stand still. She rested against an oak tree and imagined what it must be like to come from a real family. Her sister's parents had to be wonderful people. They'd taken in a baby, after all, a tiny baby whose mother had just died. They had to be true Christians.

Of course Aunt Mabel was a true Christian, and Emily was hard-pressed to describe her as wonderful, but her sister's parents were bound to be different. It was harder taking in a baby, and besides, Emily was blood kin to Aunt Mabel, even if she was half Hasbrouck, and blood was thicker than water. Aunt Mabel used to say that a lot when people would praise her for taking Emily in. Aunt Mabel never looked happy when she said it, but Emily knew she meant it because if she hadn't been family, Aunt Mabel wouldn't have looked at her twice.

Emily thought about her sister. She'd be nearly nine by now. She was sure to be pretty, with long blond curls. She'd like to read and, of course, she played the piano, but her parents probably gave her lots of toys as well. Dolls. Maybe even a doll-house. A kitten. A pony. Lots and lots of pretty dresses and more hair ribbons than a person could count.

Not that she'd be spoiled. She was too good to be spoiled. Emily was sure her sister had a loving nature, and was kind to the poor and needy. If there were any orphans in the town she lived in, Emily just knew her sister spoke to them as if they were regular children.

Emily tried picturing herself living in the same house as her sister, but it wasn't easy. The house looked just like Aunt Bessie's, only with dolls and a kitten, a baby grand instead of an upright, two maids and a cook, and a big stained-glass window in the front hallway, like they had in the Methodist church back in Madison. Then she imagined parents for her sister. The mother looked a lot like Miss Alice, only older and more respectable. The father was handsome and dashing, like the hero in the sort of novels Aunt Mabel admitted were sinful to read but read anyway. And then came Emily's sister, in a ruffled white frock, looking absolutely beautiful.

All that was easy enough. It was seeing herself in the picture that was difficult. Emily couldn't remember ever owning a really pretty dress, so the best she could do was put herself in the dress she'd worn to Aunt Mabel's funeral, only making it fit better. It had been too small for her for months, but Aunt Mabel had been too ill to think about Emily's clothes. Emily then imagined herself with her hair all grown back. That would happen soon enough. And she treated herself to a pair of pretty new shoes.

But there was no getting around the fact she wasn't perfect, not like her sister and her parents.

She looked awkward and out of place. She didn't belong.

But then Emily imagined herself at the baby grand, and suddenly she fit in. She was playing the piano, playing Mozart and Schumann, and her sister and her parents were sitting in the parlor enjoying every note. Her sister even said how wonderfully Emily played and how she hoped someday she'd play half so well.

Emily started walking again. She had a gift for music. It was the one thing her parents had truly left her. She knew vanity was a terrible sin, one she was guilty of far too much, but she couldn't help it. She knew she had a gift. The only time Aunt Mabel ever said anything nice to her was after she'd played the piano. Emily might not have parents or pretty dresses or any of the other things Harriet had, but so long as she could play the piano, she was every bit as good as they were.

Emily pictured herself in a beautiful yellow dress, with a big bow in her long curly hair, walking onstage to play the piano. Everyone she knew was in the audience. Her sister and her parents had the seats of honor, but right nearby were Mary Kate and Gracie, and way in the back, just eaten alive with jealousy, were Harriet, Florrie, and Isabella. Emily could hear the applause, and then she could hear the music. She'd start with Chopin, she decided. Chopin, then Brahms, and end with the Moonlight Sonata. She could hear every sacred note in her mind, could feel the piano keys under her fingertips. The applause was rapturous, but the music was even sweeter.

"Emily. Miss Browne wants to see you."

Emily looked up with a start. She was already back at the Home, and she hadn't even realized it.

"Thank you, Matron," Emily said. She walked straightaway into Miss Browne's office instead of going first to the dormitory to put her things away.

"Sit down, Emily," Miss Browne said.

"Yes, ma'am," Emily said.

"You've been here for a week now," Miss Browne said. "I'm sure it's been a hard week for you, but do you think you're making an adjustment to life with us?"

"Yes, ma'am," Emily said. It would hardly do to tell Miss Browne that she'd be moving out to her real family almost any day now.

"I'm glad," Miss Browne said. "It can be very difficult for a girl when her parents die or are unable to take care of her and she must come to live in a home. Of course, your parents were already dead, but the loss of your aunt must have been quite painful for you."

"Yes, ma'am," Emily said.

Miss Browne smiled at her. "Miss Webber and her mother certainly seem quite fond of you," she said. "I just received a telephone call from them asking if you might join them for Sunday dinner."

"May I?" Emily asked.

"Yes, you may," Miss Browne said. "If you behave yourself until then, that is. Saturday is work day here at Austen, and not all the girls are as cooperative as we would like. But I'm sure you'll do all the tasks assigned you."

"Yes, ma'am," Emily said.

"It's kind of the Webbers to take such an interest in you," Miss Browne said. "I trust you'll behave yourself with them and never give them a reason to regret their inviting you to their home."

"I'll be good," Emily said. "I promise."

"I'm sure you will be," Miss Browne said. "Now, Emily, how are things for you at school?"

"Fine, ma'am," Emily said.

"That's good," Miss Browne said. "You've been behaving yourself, not disturbing any of the other children?"

"Yes, ma'am," Emily said.

Miss Browne nodded. "I haven't heard otherwise from Miss Upshaw," she said. "And I'm sure if there were any cause for complaint, I would. You're respectful to your teachers?"

"Yes, ma'am," Emily said.

"Very good," Miss Browne said. "And the children. Are they leaving you alone?"

Emily paused before answering. Miss Browne didn't want to hear that Harriet was making her walk in the street. And what would Miss Browne do if Emily told her that? Tell Harriet's parents and Florrie's and Isabella's that their daughters were being mean to one of the Austen girls? Emily knew better. If Miss Browne had to choose between protecting Emily and getting material from

Florrie's father's mill for uniforms, she'd pick the material. Emily didn't even blame her. What was one orphan compared to bales of dull blue cotton?

"They're leaving me alone," Emily said.

Miss Browne looked relieved. "I'm glad to hear it," she said. "In that case, I'll continue sending Mary Kate and Gracie to school a bit early and keep you on with your breakfast duties."

"Yes, ma'am," Emily said.

"Of course, if you do have any troubles, I want you to come to me right away," Miss Browne said. "I'm here to help you, Emily. You and all our other wards."

"Thank you, Miss Browne," Emily said.

"You're excused, Emily," Miss Browne said.

Emily got up and left the office. Miss Browne was no help at all, but it didn't matter. She'd been invited to Sunday dinner at the Webbers because they'd found her sister. And that meant that in a matter of days, Emily would be living in a real home, with a real family who would love and protect her as if she were blood.

✦ Chapter 8

On Sunday, Emily put on her Sunday uniform (a gray cotton dress with a white collar and a white pinafore) and attended the Methodist church with the other Methodist Austen girls and one of the matrons. Gracie went with them, but Mary Kate turned out to be Baptist. Emily was disappointed that Miss Alice and Aunt Bessie weren't there, but she was relieved not to see Harriet, Florrie, and Isabella. The Austen girls sat in a section by themselves, but at least no one looked at them funny.

The minister gave a very fine sermon all about God helping those who helped themselves, and Emily agreed with every word. She was helping herself by finding her sister, and she knew God was smiling down His approval on her. She enjoyed singing the hymns, and felt more at home than she had anyplace since Aunt Mabel's death.

After church, she went straight to the Webbers' home. She felt proud how quickly she'd learned the streets of Oakbridge, and hoped she'd learn her sister's hometown just as easily.

"Welcome, welcome," Aunt Bessie said. "I hope you brought a big appetite with you, child."

"I did," Emily admitted. She'd spent much of Saturday fantasizing about the Sunday dinner she was about to have. Sunday dinner at the orphan home was the best meal of the week, but Emily was sure Aunt Bessie could top whatever the Home was having.

"We're having chicken and dumplings," Miss Alice told her, as though reading Emily's mind. "With peas and carrots and devil's food cake for dessert."

Emily nearly died. "Devil's food cake?" she asked.

Aunt Bessie chuckled. "I know, it's probably sinful to have anything to do with the devil on the Sabbath," she said. "But I baked it yesterday, and I'm sure the Good Lord will forgive us."

"I'm sure He will too," Emily said.

"Don't think we have cake like that every Sunday," Miss Alice said. "I don't know what it is about you, Emily, but you bring out the baker in Mother."

"I like to feed growing girls," Aunt Bessie said. "I did a good enough job on you, Alice."

"May I set the table?" Emily asked.

"You certainly may," Aunt Bessie said. "In

honor of the occasion, we're eating in the dining room."

"And using our good china, I might add," Miss Alice said, "which Father shipped from England."

"My late husband was in import/export," Aunt Bessie said. "And he loved beautiful things. This house is filled with memories of him."

"Like the piano," Emily said. "Would it be all right if I played later on?"

"We've been looking forward to it," Aunt Bessie said. "I can't recall the last time I heard a child your age play so well."

"Did your aunt leave you anything to remember her by?" Miss Alice asked as Emily carefully placed each plate on the white lace tablecloth.

"Aunt Mabel left everything to the Methodist church for missionary work," Emily replied. "Aunt Mabel was a good Christian and she wanted all the heathens to be converted."

"It doesn't seem too Christian to me to leave you penniless," Aunt Bessie said.

"Mother . . . ," Miss Alice said.

"She did the right thing," Emily said. "She took me in out of charity. My father, well, I loved him, but he was a man full of sin. He drank, you know, and he couldn't always hold on to a job. Aunt Mabel was my mother's aunt, and she never approved of my father, because he was a Hasbrouck, and they weren't as respectable as Lathrops. She didn't have to take me in. I could have ended up at an orphanage years ago when my father died. So it's only right her money went to convert the heathens."

"But she didn't leave you anything at all?" Aunt Bessie asked. "Not even a family Bible? Do you at least have pictures of your parents?"

Emily shook her head. "My papa had a picture of Mama," she said. "He'd look at it a lot and cry. But I don't know where it went after he died."

"This is a very morbid conversation for Sunday dinner," Miss Alice said. "And on such a beautiful fall day too. Let's talk about something more cheerful. Emily, tell us what you've been learning in school."

So Emily did. And during dinner they all talked. Aunt Bessie reminisced about her own school days, and Miss Alice, who had gone to the same Oakridge school as Emily, told stories about her days there. She'd even had some of the same teachers Emily now had.

Aunt Bessie and Miss Alice also told stories about Aunt Bessie's husband and all the different places he had been to: Persia, and Siam, and all the capitals of Europe. It was sad when he'd gotten sick on one of those trips, and he had just made it back to Oakridge before he'd died.

"He died without a debt," Aunt Bessie declared. "But he died without a penny as well."

That was when she'd decided to go to work. There had been telephones in Oakridge for a few years by then, and Aunt Bessie learned how to be an operator.

"I've been working for ten years now," she said. "I suppose I could have found myself a good man and remarried, but I like being independent. Have some more cake, Emily."

"Thank you," Emily said. The cake was wonderful. The whole meal had been. She felt quite full but found room for a small slice of cake.

"I went to the state teachers' college," Miss Alice said. "I thought at first I'd be a teacher . . ."

"That's what I always wanted her to be," Aunt Bessie said. "Teaching's such a worthy occupation."

"But I decided to be a librarian instead," Miss Alice said. "Luckily, Mother thinks that's pretty worthy as well."

"Not as worthy as teaching," Aunt Bessie said. "Educating young minds. But worthier than a lot of other jobs Alice might have had."

"Have you given any thought to what you want to do when you grow up, Emily?" Miss Alice asked.

"I'd like to play the piano," Emily said. "I don't know if I'm good enough to be a concert pianist, but even just to play at the moving picture shows would be wonderful. My aunt Mabel didn't approve of moving pictures, but Mrs. James, my piano teacher back in Madison, took me once and there was a piano player there. Or I could teach piano, the way Mrs. James did. I just love music so. But Miss Browne says most of the Austen girls become servants or go to work at the mill. They can't keep us past sixteen, so we can't finish our education. And they don't have a piano, or any money for us to take lessons even if there were a teacher willing to give them to us. So I suppose I'll become a housemaid. But maybe I'll work in a home that has a piano."

"Even if you do, child, chances are they won't let you play it," Aunt Bessie said. "Now I understand why it's so important for you to find your sister."

"It isn't just so I'll play the piano," Emily said. "My sister is family to me. And family is the most important thing in the world."

"I suppose it is," Aunt Bessie said. "Emily, I wasn't sure how to tell you, or truly even if I should, but I got a name and address for your sister."

"You did?" Emily said. "What's her name? Where does she live?"

"I don't rightly know your sister's name," Aunt Bessie said. "I found out her parents' name, but not hers. That never came up."

"Oh," Emily said. Wonderful though it was to know where her sister was living, she still wanted to have a real name to attach to her image.

"Let me tell you, it wasn't easy finding anything out," Aunt Bessie declared. "You didn't give me much to go on."

"Mother had to do a great deal of detective work," Miss Alice said.

"It took me all of Friday to learn what I did,"

Aunt Bessie said. "It seemed like Friday everybody was using the telephone. I can't remember such a busy day. And there were times when I had my doubts about what I was doing. You're just a child, and I wasn't sure it was right to be searching the way I was for you without hearing from someone, Miss Browne maybe, that you would be better off knowing all about your sister. But now that I think about what your future will be if you stay at Austen, I'm glad I found out what I could."

Emily couldn't understand why Aunt Bessie had had any doubts. But she also couldn't imagine any other adult, not even Mrs. James, going to so much bother for her. "Thank you, Aunt Bessie," Emily said, "for doing it for me."

"You deserve better than your lot," Aunt Bessie said. "I suppose all the Austen girls do, but at least you're one I can help out. Anyhow, I started with the Methodist church in Forestburg. Only it seems there isn't a Methodist church in Forestburg anymore. It burned down about ten years ago, and all the Methodists go to church in Winslow Falls now. I telephoned there, but the minister had retired about five years ago, and the new minister didn't know anything about you or your family."

"No, he wouldn't," Emily said. "Even if we still lived near Winslow Falls. Papa wasn't one for churchgoing. At least not after Mama died."

"I asked the minister if he knew where the old minister was, and he said he wasn't sure, it seemed to him he'd moved to Wisconsin to live with his daughter and her family, but frankly he hadn't been close to the old minister. So I asked him if he knew anybody who might know where he was, and he had to think about it, and then he said Mrs. Pierce might know; she was kin to the minister's late wife."

"It sounds so complicated," Emily said.

"Hold on," Miss Alice said. "It gets even more complicated."

"I telephoned Mrs. Pierce then," Aunt Bessie said. "And I had a lovely chat with her. My cousin married a Pierce, who turns out to be her husband's second cousin. So we're family in a roundabout way. Mrs. Pierce said the Reverend Mr. Johnson moved to Lawrence, Wisconsin, when his wife took poorly. The poor woman died two years ago, and he's stayed on with his daughter and her husband. The husband's a dentist, and very active in the Masons. As soon as I had the chance, I called Lawrence and located Mr. Johnson. He was very happy to speak with me. He'd been Methodist minister in Winslow Falls for ten years, but living in Wisconsin the way he does, he doesn't have much chance to talk about the old days."

"Did he know where my sister was?" Emily asked.

"He didn't have a clue," Aunt Bessie said. "He said he remembered burying your poor mama. It was raining that day, and your father kept crying. He remembered you at the funeral, just a tot, he said, all dressed in black and calling for her mama.

I swear, we both got a little teary thinking about it. But he didn't know what had become of your sister."

"Then how did you find out?" Emily asked.

"I asked him who might know if he didn't," Aunt Bessie said. "I explained to him how your papa had died and then your aunt Mabel, and how your sister was the only family you had left, and naturally you felt your mama would want the two of you to be together. I asked him if maybe there was a doctor in Forestburg who might know something, and he said that the rich ladies had a doctor deliver their babies, but most everybody else used the midwife, Mrs. Shirley. At least that was how it had been when he lived in Winslow Falls. So we hung up, and when I had the chance, I called Winslow Falls again, and this time I spoke to Mrs. Shirley."

"That was so kind of you," Emily said. "Making all those phone calls."

"Tell you the truth, by that time, I was determined to find your sister," Aunt Bessie said. "Picturing you at your mama's funeral made it seem real important to me. Lucky for us, nobody was having a baby, and Mrs. Shirley was free to talk. She had delivered your sister. You, too, for that matter, but she remembered your sister better because of your mama dying. Mrs. Shirley said your mama was in a real bad way by the time she got there, and it was all she could do to save the poor baby's life. Your father got the doctor, but your mama died a few hours later. Mrs. Shirley still feels bad about it. She said she's lost very few of her patients over the years, and each one feels like an open wound to her."

"Did she know where my sister was?" Emily asked.

"Not exactly," Aunt Bessie said. "She said a neighbor woman took the baby in—your poor father was in no state to care for a newborn—and she didn't have any contact with your family after that. I asked if she knew the neighbor woman's name, and she thought really hard and said it was probably Mrs. Fields, because she lived right close to your family, and that was the kind of thing she did. So I called Mrs. Fields as soon as I had the chance. We had quite a nice chat, too. Her son went to school with Alice's Tim."

"Robert Fields?" Alice asked. "You didn't tell me that, Mother."

"I must've forgotten," Aunt Bessie said. "Anyway, Mrs. Fields hadn't taken the baby in, since her own children had whooping cough at the time, but she knew who had. It was Mrs. Stoddard, who also lived near you and your family, and was a real good friend to your mother. Mrs. Fields was sure if anybody knew where that poor baby had gone, it would be Mrs. Stoddard."

"And did she?" Emily asked.

"Almost," Aunt Bessie said. "She said she took care of the baby for over a week, until she got some strength and your poor father could decide what he was going to do about her. Meantime, her cousin Maude mentioned a family she knew that was just about frantic to have a baby, nice respectable people, who had had three babes of their own all die at birth. Mrs. Stoddard felt terrible, she couldn't remember the family's name, but she told me where I could find Cousin Maude. So I telephoned her, and she remembered it all as if it was yesterday. The tiny little baby, and your father just devastated by his wife's death, and you, poor motherless child. When I told her about your papa's death, and then your aunt Mabel, Maude was near tears herself. She said she didn't know the people who took your sister in that well, but they went to church together, and she knew them to be good Christian people who had suffered great pain from the deaths of their own babies. So she took it upon herself to tell them about the newborn infant, and the father who had a three-year-old to take care of, and they paid a call on Mrs. Stoddard, and agreed your sister was a healthy respectable baby. Then they paid a call to your papa, and he said they could raise the child as their own. Maude said he was very bitter about the baby, since it was her that caused your poor mama to die. He never even saw the babe. I suppose papers were signed, making it all legal, but the baby went from the Stoddards to this new family. Maude said their name was Smiley, and a couple of years after they adopted your sister, they moved to Longview."

"Longview," Emily said. "That isn't so very far from here."

"Forty miles or so," Aunt Bessie said. "I called the telephone operator, and sure enough, the Smileys live right outside of Longview. I didn't telephone them since it wasn't my place, but I have their address if you want to write to them."

"Of course, I do," Emily said. "You really found her? My sister lives in Longview?"

"Why don't you write to her now?" Miss Alice asked.

"Better still, write to her folks," Aunt Bessie said. "It's going to come as a shock to them, learning about how your father died and all, and they should know so they can tell it to your sister. She is only eight, after all."

"That's right," Emily said. "I will. I'll write to them." But then she looked stricken. "I can't," she said. "I don't have an envelope or a stamp."

Miss Alice laughed. "That we can help you with," she said. "Mother, get that pretty stationery I gave you for your birthday. Emily deserves the best."

"Could I have them write back to me care of the library?" Emily asked. "I don't want anybody at the orphan home to know yet. Not until things work out."

"I don't see why not," Miss Alice replied. "Mother, get the stationery, and Emily and I will decide just how to tell the Smileys that their daughter's sister wants to say hello!"

+I+ Chapter 9

Miss Browne was right, Emily thought on Friday as she helped Miss Alice shelve books. The first week was definitely hardest at Austen. This second week hadn't been too bad at all.

She still wasn't comfortable with the noise and lack of privacy at the Home, but since she could tell herself now that it wouldn't last that much longer, she could bear it. School was still fun, and she enjoyed eating lunch every day with Mary Kate and Gracie. It had been a long time since Emily had friends. But best of all was Miss Alice, Aunt Bessie, and the piano.

Emily had taken to going to the library after school each day. It gave her something to do and someone to talk with, and it meant she'd be right at hand when the letter came from her sister. No letter yet, but maybe tomorrow, maybe on Monday.

Twice during the week, Miss Alice invited Emily to have supper with her and her mother. The meals hadn't been nearly as fancy as the ones Aunt Bessie had made the week before, but the atmosphere was homey, and after supper Emily was allowed to play the piano. Emily missed the lessons she'd had, and her daily practice, but any time at the piano made her feel more alive, more human. Emily knew she'd miss Aunt Bessie and Miss Alice when she moved in with her sister, but she knew how much she owed them and had every intention of staying in touch. Maybe Miss Alice would invite her to her wedding.

Really, the only bad thing in her life now was walking to school every day by herself and running into Harriet, Florrie, and Isabella. As soon as she saw them, Emily hopped into the street. They laughed at her and called her nasty names, but Aunt Mabel had always said everyone had a cross to bear, and Emily supposed the humiliation she suffered was hers. It was probably punishment for the pride she felt when she played the piano. Besides, as long as she did what Harriet and the others wanted her to do, they didn't complain, and Emily didn't have to ask Miss Browne to give her an afternoon task. With her afternoons free, she could work at the library and go afterward to the Webbers' home and play their piano. That was worth the shame she felt, especially since it was only a matter of time before her sister's new family took her in.

"There, that's done," Miss Alice said Friday afternoon as they put away the last of the books. "I don't know how I managed before you moved to town, Emily."

"I'm sure you did fine," Emily said.

Miss Alice shook her head. "You're the best worker I've ever known," she said. "I know you want to be a pianist, but if that doesn't work out, maybe you should become a librarian. I think you'd make a wonderful one."

"Thank you," Emily said. If being a pianist didn't work out, she suspected she'd be a servant somewhere, but it was fun to think about being a librarian, just like Miss Alice.

"There are a couple of things I'd like to talk to you about," Miss Alice said. "In private. Let's use my office, all right, Emily?"

"Sure," Emily said. She doubted it was bad news, and she knew it wasn't about her sister, since the first thing she always asked was if there had been any word, and Miss Alice wouldn't lie. And she'd been so helpful to Miss Alice, she didn't think the librarian was going to tell her to stop coming. Miss Browne had no reason to stop her either. So Emily told herself not to be nervous, although her stomach did clench just a little bit.

Miss Alice closed the door of her office and she and Emily sat down. When Miss Alice smiled, Emily relaxed.

"You've been coming every day this week,"

Miss Alice said. "And you've worked here every one of those days."

"I like working here," Emily said. "And you said I was doing all right."

"Oh you are," Miss Alice said. "And I want you to keep working here. But it isn't fair that you do all that work and not get paid for it."

"You don't have to pay me," Emily said. "They don't pay us at the Home for the work we do there. Aunt Mabel never paid."

"But you get room and board there," Miss Alice said. "The library doesn't give you either of those."

"But you let me play your piano," Emily said.

"Mother and I love hearing you play the piano," Miss Alice said. "It brings back many wonderful memories of Father. And that has nothing to do with the work you do here. I thought twenty-five cents a day for that. It's not a lot, but at least it's a token payment for all the work you've done. And you've worked seven days, so we owe you a dollar seventy-five. Which I have here." She opened up the drawer of her desk and handed Emily a silver dollar and three quarters.

Emily stared at the money. "I never had so much money in my life," she said. "Thank you." She knew Miss Alice didn't have to pay her, and she suspected the twenty-five cents a day was coming from Miss Alice's salary. But it wasn't charity. Emily had worked hard at the library, and just because you enjoyed what you were doing didn't mean it wasn't work.

"Do you want me to hold the money for you until Monday?" Miss Alice asked. "You could open a bank account then, to keep the money in."

Emily loved the feel of the coins in her pocket. "I'll hold on to the money," she said. "Nobody at the Home ever has any, so nobody'll know to steal it."

Miss Alice smiled. "Fine," she said. "As long as you're comfortable with it, it's all yours."

"Thank you," Emily said. "Thank you for everything. Would you like me to go back to work now?"

Miss Alice glanced at the clock on her desk. "There is something else," she said. "Maybe I should let my mother talk to you about it first. I don't know. I think I will."

"What is it, ma'am?" Emily asked. Miss Alice had gotten all serious-looking, and Emily grew nervous again.

"Mother and I have been trying to work something out so you could spend more time with us," Miss Alice said. "Miss Browne says if you stay at the Home on Saturdays to do your tasks, you can spend Saturday night and Sundays with us. Would you like that?"

"I'd like it a lot," Emily said. "Could I start this weekend?"

Miss Alice smiled apologetically. "That's why I should have waited before discussing this with you," she said. "My mother and I are going to be out of town this weekend. As a matter of fact, as soon as I close up the library, I'm picking Mother up. We've visiting Tim for the weekend. So your visits will have to start next week, if you don't mind waiting."

"By next week I'll be living with my sister," Emily said. "I'm sure of it. But thank you anyway."

There was a knock on the office door. "Come in," Miss Alice said.

Much to Emily's surprise, it was Gracie. "I was looking for Emily," she said.

"You found her," Miss Alice said. "Good-bye, Emily. I'll see you on Monday."

"Yes, ma'am," Emily said. "Thank you again." She felt the four coins in her pocket, and relished the sensation of having money all her own. She'd start that bank account, the way Miss Alice had suggested, but she'd use the money to buy a present for her sister. She didn't know what yet, but it would be something wonderful, something so perfect it would make up for the fact that Emily was coming from an orphan home to live with the Smileys. She almost wished she could work at the library a week or two longer, to earn enough money to buy something really fine.

"What are you doing here?" she asked Gracie, as the two of them walked out of the library.

"I came to take out a book," Gracie said. "I like reading. You know that. Besides, I never get to see you anymore. I thought this way we could walk home together."

"That'll be nice," Emily said. She thought about telling Gracie about the money but decided not to. Why make Gracie jealous? She and the other girls at the Home were already envious of Emily for having so many meals at the Webbers'. The Home had a policy of encouraging its girls to make friends with the people in town, but few of the townspeople wanted to have anything to do with them. Emily knew how fortunate she was, and she didn't think it would be nice to show off to Gracie about it.

"Mary Kate didn't come with me," Gracie said, as the girls began their walk back. "I said to her, 'Mary Kate, you're never going to make anything of yourself if you don't read and do your school-work,' but she just said once she got bosoms it wouldn't matter if she couldn't read too good. Mary Kate is sure counting a lot on those bosoms."

"Mary Kate is pretty," Emily said. "I bet once she gets bosoms she will be able to be an actress."

"Lots of the foundlings are pretty," Gracie said. "Their mothers are pretty, and that's why they get seduced and succumb to temptation. The same thing is going to happen to Mary Kate if she doesn't watch out."

"She'll watch out," Emily said. "Mary Kate isn't going to leave a baby on the orphan home steps."

"I'm glad you're so sure," Gracie said. "But I

bet they said the same thing about her mother once."

Emily laughed. It was a beautiful fall day, she had money in her pocket, and any day now she was going to hear from her sister with an invitation to move in with her and become part of her family. Let Gracie worry about Mary Kate and her bosoms. Emily didn't feel like worrying about a thing.

"Look at that. It's those stupid hogs."

Emily whirled around. Walking toward her and Gracie were Harriet, Florrie, and Isabella. How could good fortune turn so rapidly into bad?

Pride goeth before a fall, she could hear Aunt Mabel say. That was always one of her favorites, right along with a fool and his money are soon parted. In spite of herself, Emily felt in her pocket for her coins.

"Get out of our way, hogs," Florrie said. "These sidewalks are for the respectable people in this town."

"Not little bastards like you," Harriet said.

Florrie and Isabella giggled nervously. "I don't believe you said that word," Isabella said. "My mother would wash my mouth out with soap if she ever heard me saying it."

"It may be a bad word, but it's true," Harriet said. "Why do you think hogs end up in an orphan asylum? Decent girls from decent families don't live there. Just bastard hogs, who don't belong on our sidewalks."

"That isn't true," Gracie said. "My parents were just as married as yours are, Harriet. So were Emily's."

"Will you get off the sidewalk, or do I have to call the police?" Isabella asked. "My father said he'd send any of you hogs to jail if he found out you were bothering us again. He can do it, too, because he's a judge and he runs your stupid orphan home. If he thinks you belong in jail, then it's off to jail you go." She laughed at the thought.

"I don't believe you," Gracie said. "This sidewalk is just as much ours as it is yours. Isn't it, Emily?"

"We have this hog well trained," Harriet said, giving Emily a little shove. "She knows she has to walk in the street. We don't even have to tell her to anymore."

"Is that true?" Gracie asked. "Do you really walk in the street?"

"She does just what we tell her to," Isabella said. "Don't you, hog?"

"You should be ashamed of yourself, Emily," Gracie said. "Walking in the street, like you were some kind of animal."

Emily didn't know who she was angrier at. She wanted to tell Gracie to stop scolding her almost as much as she wished Harriet, Isabella, and Florrie would fall off the face of the earth.

It didn't matter, she told herself. She was only there a little while longer, until her sister wrote to say she should move in with her. And she couldn't risk getting into trouble. Isabella was right. If Judge Cosgrove wanted Emily in jail, then that's where she'd end up.

So what if Gracie didn't respect her? She didn't need Gracie's respect or her friendship. Once you had family, you didn't need friends.

"It isn't important," she said to Gracie. "You get there just as fast on the street as on the sidewalk." As if to prove her point, she stepped off the sidewalk and onto the street. She tried not to mind when Harriet and her friends laughed at their triumph.

"It is too important," Gracie said. "These girls don't own Oakridge. Their fathers don't even own it. I may live in an orphan home, but that's only until my mother can come get me. And she wouldn't approve of my walking on the street. It isn't safe, and it certainly isn't ladylike."

"Ladylike!" Harriet said. "Ladylike. The hog thinks she's a lady."

"The hog thinks she's as good as we are," Isabella said. "At least the bald hog has learned her place. Now we'll have to teach it to this one as well."

"You're not going to teach me anything," Gracie said. "Now if you'll just excuse me, I'll continue with my walk."

"Gracie, just come down here," Emily said. "Don't argue."

"I will too argue," Gracie said. "Have these

110

girls been making you walk in the street every day?"

"It's all right," Emily said. "I don't mind."

"You ought to," Gracie said. "This isn't just about you. It's about all the Austen girls. Even the foundlings. We have just as many rights as anybody else."

"I'm getting tired of you, hog," Harriet said. "Get off this sidewalk before I have to push you off."

"No," Gracie said. "Let me pass and then you won't have to see me again until Monday."

"Push her, Harriet," Florrie said. "Teach the hog her place."

"Push her," Isabella said. "She'll end up in the gutter anyway. There's where her mother was from."

"My mother is a lady!" Gracie cried. "Don't you dare say another word about my mother."

"Just step down here," Emily said. "Please, Gracie. Don't make them call the police."

"I will not," Gracie said. "This is my sidewalk just as much as it's theirs. You should be on it too, Emily."

"Push her now!" Florrie screamed. "Get her off my sidewalk!"

"Guttersnipe," Harriet said. "I'll teach you your place."

"Just you try," Gracie said, and stood her ground.

111

"Come on, Isabella," Harriet said. "This hog is going to be heavy."

Harriet and Isabella both stepped to Gracie's side, and pushed her together. Their force shoved Gracie almost into the middle of the street. Florrie stood there laughing.

"Now the sidewalk belongs to decent people," Isabella said.

"Gracie," Emily said. "Get up."

"Let her lie there," Harriet said. "Let her crawl to the gutter."

"Gracie," Emily said. Gracie was very still. Emily looked at her more carefully and saw what must have happened. There was a rock on the street, and Gracie had hit her head against it when she fell. "Gracie. Wake up."

Gracie didn't move.

"Get a doctor," Emily said. "Don't just stand there. Get a doctor!"

Harriet and Isabella stared in horror, and then began running away. Florrie looked at them, and began hobbling after them. "Wait for me," she cried. "Don't leave me here."

"Help!" Emily screamed. "Somebody help us!"

The doors to the houses began to open, and a few people came out to see what had happened. Harriet and Isabella could no longer be seen, but Florrie was only a few feet away.

"I'll lift her," a man said. Emily didn't even know where he came from, or any of the other people who were now crowding about. Where had they been a minute before? Why were they only now coming to assist them?

"Is she breathing?" one of the people asked.

The man who had lifted Gracie put his head to her chest. "I don't think so," he said.

"Get her to Doc Edwards fast," another man said.

"Gracie!" Emily screamed.

"Just what happened here?" a policeman asked. "Who is this girl?"

"She's from the Home," a woman said. "See her uniform?"

The policeman blew his whistle. "Clear the way," he said. "Let's get her to the doctor."

"Let me go with her," Emily said. "She's my friend. I have to go with her."

"Wait a second, here comes Doc Edwards," someone said. And sure enough, a man dressed in a white coat came racing out of one of the houses.

"Clear the way for the doc," the policeman said.

"Put her on that bench," the doctor said. The man holding Gracie laid her down gently.

The doctor put on his stethoscope and listened to Gracie's heart. Next he felt for her pulse. And then, in a near whisper he asked if any of the ladies had a mirror on them.

One of the women ran back to her house and came out carrying a small pocket mirror. Doc Edwards put it almost on top of Gracie's mouth and then moved it gently away from her.

"She's dead," he said.

"What?" Emily said. "What are you talking about? She can't be dead."

"She hit herself hard on that rock when she fell," the man who had carried Gracie said.

"What's a rock doing on the street anyway?" one of the women asked.

"It must've come from the quarry wagon," someone else said. "They're always dropping rocks on this street."

"Something should be done about that," a man said. "This time it's a kid from the Home, but next time it could be one of us."

"She must have tripped when she was crossing the street," a man said. "Is that what happened, Florrie?"

Florrie nodded. "Yes, Mr. Davis," she said. "That girl, and this other one here from the Home, they were teasing me, because I'm a cripple, and then they were running away after they said their cruel things, and the one who fell, she just tripped over her own feet, and the next thing we knew, she was lying there."

"That's not true," Emily said. She reached for the policeman to make sure he was listening. "What she said isn't true. Harriet and Isabella were here too, and they pushed Gracie. She didn't fall. She was pushed."

"Are you talking about Harriet Dale and Isabella Cosgrove?" Mr. Davis asked. "Are you saying those girls had anything to do with this?"

Emily looked at Gracie's lifeless body. "Yes, sir, I am," she said. "They pushed her onto the street and now she's . . ." But she couldn't finish the sentence.

"She's lying," Florrie said. "You know those orphan home girls. They lie and steal from us all the time. They ought to be sent to jail instead of living on our charity."

"I did see two girls running away from here," one of the women said.

"They were running for help," Florrie said. "They were here, trying to protect me, but there wasn't anything they could do. That girl, the one who's making all those false accusations, she pushed me just last week. Because I'm a cripple. Ask Miss Upshaw. And Harriet and Isabella saw that other one fall and they ran to get a doctor. You told them to!" she shouted at Emily. "You begged them to get a doctor and now you're lying and saying it's their fault."

"They weren't running toward Doc Edwards," the woman said. "That wasn't the direction I saw them going."

"That's because Doc Edwards isn't the orphan home doctor," Florrie said. "They were probably going to the Home, to tell them what had happened. Besides, it doesn't matter. She died right away. She must have."

"She did that," Doc Edwards said. "Just like a blow to the head. I've seen it happen before that way. The head lands just the wrong way, and you die instantly."

"They pushed her," Emily said. "I swear, they pushed her."

Florrie began to cry. "Mr. Davis, make her stop telling those awful lies," she said. "She's a mean bad girl, and she was calling me terrible names, and I'm lucky it isn't me lying dead in that street."

The crowd looked at Florrie and at Emily. "I'd say she got what she deserved," one of the men said. "Picking on a crippled girl."

"Those orphan girls are wild," a woman said. "I don't like it that they go to school with our children at all."

"Please," Emily said to the policeman. "Please listen to me. She's lying. Harriet and Isabella pushed her. They killed her."

"Nobody killed anybody," the policeman said. "It was an accident. Right, Doc?"

"Right," the doctor said. "Just a terrible senseless accident. The poor child undoubtedly tripped and hit her head against that rock. She was probably running, and that would account for the force of her head against it."

"She was running," Florrie said. "She was running away because she knew she'd get in trouble for saying such awful things to me."

"Anyone who would pick on a cripple deserves what she gets," one of the women said. "Someone had better call that Home and tell them what their wards are up to."

"You're not listening!" Emily cried. "They pushed her!"

But the crowd had already begun to disperse. Doc Edwards was standing next to the bench where Gracie had been laid to rest, and he kept shaking his head. "Terrible accident," he said.

The policeman took Emily by her arm. "We've had trouble with the orphan girls in this town in the past," he said. "I'd think carefully about what kind of lies you go around telling about decent families."

"It isn't a lie," Emily said. "Why won't you believe me? It isn't a lie."

Florrie kept crying, and several of the people surrounded her protectively. "No-good trash," one of them shouted at Emily.

"Gracie!" Emily screamed, but the policeman pulled her away from her friend, away from the crowd that was getting angrier and angrier at her accusations.

"Keep quiet," he said to Emily as he pushed her through the crowd. "Stop your lies and keep quiet from now on if you know what's good for you."

✤ Chapter 10

At supper that night, Miss Browne made an announcement to the Austen girls. She almost never was seen at suppertime, so her very appearance indicated the importance of what she had to say.

"As some of you may have heard, there was a terrible accident involving one of our girls," she declared. "Gracie Dodge, one of our older girls, died this afternoon."

There was an immediate buzz in the room.

Miss Browne held up her hand for silence. "Talk is not allowed during mealtimes," she said. "And this is no exception. Although we don't know all the facts yet, it appears Gracie tripped and her head hit a rock. She died instantly."

Emily looked at Mary Kate, and could see her friend was battling tears. She hadn't known Mary Kate was capable of crying.

"Although we must all feel great loss at Gracie's passing, we should rejoice that she is now in Heaven, in the loving arms of Jesus," Miss Browne said. "Gracie was a good girl. She has earned her heavenly reward."

Most of the girls were crying by then. Even the matrons were sniffling.

"There will be a memorial service for Gracie tomorrow after supper," Miss Browne said. "The rest of the day will be no different than usual. This Home must carry on in spite of Gracie's passing. As soon as Emily Hasbrouck is finished with supper, I want to see her in my office. Thank you."

Everyone turned to look at Emily. She made a point of finishing her food in stony silence. When the girls were dismissed, she went to Miss Browne's office.

"Come in, Emily," Miss Browne said, closing the door. "Sit down. We have a great deal to talk about."

"Yes, ma'am," Emily said.

"I know you and Gracie were friends," Miss Browne said. "I'm sorry for your loss."

"Thank you, ma'am," Emily said.

"I also know you were there when Gracie died," Miss Browne said. "It must have been dreadfully upsetting for you."

"Yes, ma'am," Emily said.

"Do you want to tell me just what happened?" Miss Browne asked.

Emily didn't, not really. But she knew it

wouldn't be right to lie, not fair somehow to Gracie. "Those girls," she said. "Harriet and the others. The ones that were teasing us. They were there, and Harriet and Isabella pushed Gracie onto the street. Florrie told them to. And Gracie fell and hit her head, I guess. And then everybody came out and Gracie was dead."

"Are you sure that's what happened?" Miss Browne asked.

"Yes, ma'am," Emily said. "That's exactly what happened."

"I've heard from the other girls' parents," Miss Browne said. "They telephoned me individually when they heard that you were telling that story. They say their daughters have a different version, that you and Gracie were tormenting Florrie and became afraid and ran away. And when Gracie turned to run, she tripped, and that was how she fell."

"That's a lie," Emily said. "They pushed Gracie."

Miss Browne sighed. "There are no witnesses," she said. "No one has come forward to say what happened. It's your word against theirs."

"Gracie never tormented anybody," Emily said. "You knew Gracie. She wasn't mean."

"I know that's how she seemed to us," Miss Browne said. "But you must understand, Florrie is a very sensitive girl. It's been quite hard on her, having a crippled leg. Perhaps you and Gracie said something, not meaning for it to be cruel, but it seemed that way to Florrie?"

"No, ma'am," Emily said. "Gracie didn't say anything mean."

"Did you?" Miss Browne asked. "I know those girls have teased you. Did you possibly say something back to them that Florrie could have interpreted as an attack?"

Emily tried to remember what she'd said. She could picture herself in the street, terrified the girls would provoke them into a fight and Emily would end up in jail. Emily groveled, just the way they wanted her to.

"I didn't say anything," Emily said. "I told Gracie to get in the street with me, but she wouldn't."

"In the street?" Miss Browne asked. "Why did you say that to Gracie?"

"Because that's where they wanted us to be," Emily said. "I've been walking there all week so they wouldn't push me. They said we weren't good enough to use their sidewalks. But Gracie said she had just as much right to the sidewalk as they did, so they pushed her." Emily paused for a moment. "They called her a bastard," she whispered. "That made Gracie mad and she said she was a lady and they laughed at her and pushed her."

"Oh, Emily," Miss Browne said. "Are you sure that's what happened?"

"That's exactly what happened," Emily said. "It's my fault Gracie died. I should have fought

121

Harriet. But when I did last week, I got into trouble and you told me not to. You said we needed their charity. So I walked in the street and I didn't say anything when they called me names. But Gracie didn't understand, and I couldn't explain it to her, and they pushed her. And that's what happened. Honest, Miss Browne. That's exactly what happened."

Miss Browne shook her head. "I'm sure you think you're telling the truth," she said.

"I am telling the truth," Emily said.

"Don't interrupt," Miss Browne said. "I know you're upset and angry, but that doesn't give you the right to interrupt."

"I'm sorry, ma'am," Emily said. She wasn't sorry at all.

"Look at me, Emily," Miss Browne said. "Three girls from the best families in town say you and Gracie were teasing one of them, a crippled girl at that, and Gracie brought the accident upon herself by trying to run away. Miss Upshaw has also been interviewed, and she said she witnessed you and Gracie and Mary Kate tormenting Florrie. When the policeman spoke to me, I had to admit that you'd been punished for that very incident last week. Isabella's father said he had shown a policeman the letter of apology you'd written, where you admitted pushing his daughter. No one saw what happened except you and the girls, and no one is going to believe your version, whether it's the truth or not."

"But that isn't fair," Emily said. "That isn't right."

"No it isn't," Miss Browne said. "But that's the way of the world. Eleven-year-old orphan girls cannot stand up to mayors and judges and mill owners. As it is, Judge Cosgrove suggested to me that you be turned away from the Austen Home. I'm hoping to be able to convince him otherwise, but in the meantime, you cannot go around accusing his daughter of killing Gracie."

"I don't care," Emily said. "Send me to a city asylum. It's got to be better than here."

"Oh, no, it won't be," Miss Browne said. "Austen may not be a high-quality finishing school, but it's a hundred times better than the kind of place Judge Cosgrove wants to see you in. We have clean clothes and decent food and mattresses for our girls. There's heat in the winter, and schooling, and we don't beat our girls when they misbehave. I know these past few weeks have been horribly difficult for you, but you couldn't survive in a city asylum. It would kill you in a month, spiritually if not physically. I'll do everything in my power to see you don't end up in one. But you have to help me."

"By lying?" Emily asked.

"By not telling your story, truth or lie," Miss Browne said.

"But that isn't right," Emily said. "That isn't fair to Gracie."

"Gracie is in Heaven," Miss Browne said. "And I'm sure she forgives you."

Emily wasn't sure at all.

"I'm going to send you to the isolation room," Miss Browne said. "You'll stay there for the weekend. I don't want you telling your story to the girls here. It will only upset them, and it will accomplish nothing."

"What about Gracie?" Emily asked.

Miss Browne sighed. "We'll bury her tomorrow," she said. "The board of trustees wants her burial to be small, private, and fast. The Austen girls who die, and Gracie is only the second since I came here, are laid to rest in the potter's field. The Reverend Mr. Johnson will officiate, and I will be there representing Austen. The memorial service Saturday night will be for all of us. I'm afraid you won't be allowed to attend, since I don't want the girls speculating about why you're in isolation. It's best if they simply think you don't feel well."

"You can't do that," Emily said.

"I can and will do whatever I think is best for this Home," Miss Browne said. "I know you're upset that you won't be able to attend the memorial service, but I can't have eighty girls speculating about what happened on that street today and turning to you for answers."

"That's not what I meant," Emily said. "I meant about burying Gracie in potter's field. What would her mother say?"

124

"Whose mother?" Miss Browne asked. "What are you talking about?"

"Gracie's mother," Emily replied. "She'll want to take Gracie back with her, bury her in her family plot. If you bury her in potter's field, how will her mother ever find her?"

"I don't understand," Miss Browne asked. "Why do you keep talking about Gracie's mother?"

"Because Gracie was waiting for her to come back," Emily said. "Everyone knew that. Gracie's mother told her she'd be back for her one day."

Miss Browne covered her face with her hand, and for one horrible moment Emily thought she was going to cry. Emily didn't know what she would do if Miss Browne cried.

"No one knows where Gracie's mother is," Miss Browne finally said. "When Gracie was seven, a family wanted to adopt her. We wrote to Gracie's mother to see if she'd give permission, but the letter came back to us undelivered. Gracie's mother may be dead, or she may have simply moved on. So many of our girls are like that, with a parent who won't sign away legal rights but makes no effort to stay in touch. And the girls keep dreaming about their mothers and fathers, waiting for them to come and rescue them, and they're never going to be rescued. Gracie had no mother. She had no one but us, and we let her down. We let her die." Miss Browne did begin crying then, sobbing.

Emily stared at her, and then, without even asking permission, left her office. Matron was standing at the door and, without saying a word, escorted Emily to the isolation room.

Emily spent a horrible night Friday dreaming over and over of Gracie falling, Gracie being pushed. In her dreams Aunt Mabel kept saying "Pride goeth before a fall." Sometimes it was one of the girls who said it, and sometimes they just laughed. Sometimes it was Emily they pushed, and Gracie stood with them crying. By the time dawn arrived, Emily felt she'd had that dream a hundred times over, and she longed never to sleep again.

Saturday the girls got their clean uniforms, and even with Emily in isolation, hers was delivered to her. Emily could hear the key turning to unlock her door, but when she opened it there was no one there, just the uniform neatly folded on the floor.

Emily picked the uniform up and closed the door. It was locked almost immediately. They wouldn't let her have contact with anybody, Emily realized. They didn't even want her to tell the truth to the matrons.

Emily put on the uniform, and then took the dollar and seventy-five cents, which she'd slept with the night before, and put it in the dress pocket. When she did, she felt a folded piece of paper.

It was a rainy, gray day, but there was enough light from the window for Emily to read the note.

I am running away tomorow before school. I cant stay here without Gracie. I dont care I dont have buzums. Ill get them later.

Mary Kate

Im sorry to leave you. You are nice. But Gracie was my true friend.

Emily refolded the note and put it back in her pocket. She wondered if she should tell someone of Mary Kate's plan. What was she going to do, all alone with no family and no bosoms? How could she possibly survive?

At least I have a family, Emily told herself. She curled up in the corner of the room and thought once again about her sister with the long blond curls and the pony and the piano. She imagined herself in the picture, wearing the same kind of pretty dresses Harriet always wore. No, prettier. A ruffled pink organdy dress with a matching pink hairbow. Her sister's parents, Emily's new parents, stood behind their two daughters. They looked powerful and respectable. They had never let any harm come to Emily's sister, and now that they loved Emily as well and thought of her as their daughter, they would protect her, educate her, raise her to be a proper member of society.

Emily spent Saturday thinking about her new family. She thought about Gracie as well, and the mother Gracie had so counted on, who couldn't even be notified of her daughter's death. She thought about Mary Kate, who was going to run away and take her chances on the streets rather than stay behind at Austen without the only person she'd ever loved.

And Emily thought hard about Harriet, Isabella, and Florrie. With their money and their families, they could buy a lie and turn it into the truth.

Emily knew that Harriet and Isabella hadn't meant to kill Gracie. They didn't know the rock was there, could not possibly have imagined that Gracie would land on it and die. They weren't murderers, just cruel, spiteful girls who wanted to prove how much better they were than girls like Gracie. Girls like Emily. Girls whose very food and clothing were dependent on the charity of the Dales, the Sheldons, the Cosgroves.

Emily took out Mary Kate's note, and then her dollar and seventy-five cents. That was all she owned in the world, she realized. Her mother had left her nothing, not even a sister. Her father had left her nothing, not even a picture of her family. Aunt Mabel had left her nothing, not even the Lathrop name. They had all in their own ways loved her, but they had left her nothing. Even Gracie's mother, who had deserted her, had left her daughter a dream.

God helps those who help themselves, Emily told herself. She could picture Gracie in Heaven, surrounded by angels. She'd pictured her mother that way hundreds of times, although she'd always had a harder time imagining her father up there as well. As for Aunt Mabel, Emily wasn't sure Heaven would be quite good enough for her standards.

But Gracie was there, and so was Emily's mother, and they both had it in their hearts to forgive Emily her many sins. They were good, and they loved Emily.

Too bad they're dead, she thought. She could use someone to love her right then.

Emily swallowed hard. The devil finds mischief for idle hands, she told herself. Aunt Mabel always said that when she found Emily with nothing to do. And Emily knew she was right, knew that she was having horrible wicked thoughts because she was all alone with nothing to do but stare out a window and listen to the rain.

She had someone to love her. She had a sister just forty miles away. A sister her mother never wanted her to be parted from. Her own flesh and blood. And she had that one dollar and seventy-five cents, so all she had to do was buy a train ticket to Longview, find the Smileys, and introduce herself. True, she hadn't heard from them yet, but they had undoubtedly already written. Perhaps the letter had arrived this morning, but Miss Alice was away and couldn't tell her. Emily wished Miss Alice and Aunt Bessie were in town. They'd believe her, even if nobody else did. Then a terrible thought crossed her mind. She imagined herself walking to school all alone on Monday. There she was, just a couple of blocks from school, and there were Harriet, Florrie, and Isabella, the same as they always were.

What would they do to her on Monday, Emily wondered. They had killed Gracie, and they knew she knew it. They didn't want her around. What would they do to her?

Emily told herself she was being foolish to think they might kill her. Gracie's death had been an accident, the girls weren't murderers, and it was even possible that truly they felt sorry over what they had done.

But she knew they didn't want her around, and she knew Miss Browne was right. She didn't want to be sent to an orphan asylum in the city. Worse yet, Judge Cosgrove might find some way to have her sent to jail, the way Harriet and the others had threatened. The judge was on the board of trustees, along with Harriet's father, and Miss Browne would have to obey any orders they gave her about what to do with Emily.

Miss Alice would probably be able to find Emily if she were in a city home somewhere, and maybe the Smileys would still take her in, just because she was their daughter's sister. But if she ended up in jail, there would be no way to rescue her. And if she'd been afraid of jail before Gracie died, Emily was now terrified of it.

A dollar and seventy-five cents. It wasn't a fortune, but it should be enough to buy a train ticket to Longview. The more Emily thought about it, the more sure she was there was a letter waiting for her at the library, inviting her to live with her sister. True, it would be best if she could wait for the Smileys to come and get her. But given the circumstances, if Emily wanted God to help her, she was going to have to help herself and join her sister as soon as she possibly could.

✢ Chapter 11

Monday morning Emily was freed from isolation in time to help set the breakfast tables. She did her work silently, looking at no one, not even Mary Kate, as the girls entered the room and ate their morning meal. After breakfast, she cleared the tables, then returned to the dormitory to get her schoolbooks.

She slipped out of the Home without seeing Miss Browne, which was a relief, and walked a few blocks toward the school. When she was sure no one had spotted her, she backtracked, and walked on side streets until she was safely out of the town limits.

The town nearest Oakbridge was Lincoln, and that was five miles away. It was a long walk, and Emily soon tired of carrying her schoolbooks. What did they matter? she thought. When she lived in Longview with the Smileys she'd get new schoolbooks anyway. New books, and new clothes (no more uniforms), and a new life. A new name, too, probably. Her sister's last name was Smiley now, and soon hers would be as well.

The temperature had cooled off since Friday, she noted, which helped. Emily didn't think she'd ever walked five miles before, but when she'd lived with Aunt Mabel she'd run errands all the time, to the store or the library, as well as going for her piano lessons, and Aunt Mabel had lived a couple of miles from town. Emily had decided against taking a train from Oakbridge to Longview, in case anyone at the orphan home decided to look for her. They might ask at the train station if she'd been there. But they would never think to ask at Lincoln, and that made the long walk worth it. Once the Smileys took her in, Emily would let Miss Browne know where she was. But she didn't want to get caught before she made it to Longview.

Emily hummed hymns as she walked, and thought about her sister and her new family. She thought about how excited Aunt Bessie and Miss Alice would be for her when they learned about her new home. She felt in her pocket for her money, and fingered Mary Kate's note as well. What different lives she and Mary Kate would be leading. She could only hope Mary Kate would be safe and happy.

A couple of times Emily thought of Gracie, but

the thoughts made her sad and angry and she told herself not to dwell on them. Gracie was in Heaven, and there was nothing Emily could do for her anymore. She thought about Harriet, Florrie, and Isabella. Someday she'd be rich and she'd come back to Oakridge and make them pay for what they'd done. She could hear Aunt Mabel saying "Vengeance is mine, saith the Lord," but that didn't take away any of the pleasure of thinking about what she might someday do to Harriet and the others. In the meantime, she made a point of walking on the sidewalk and not on the streets.

Emily found the railroad station in Lincoln easily enough. "I want to go to Longview," she said at the ticket window. "When's the next train?"

"You're in luck," the clerk said. "It leaves in about ten minutes."

Emily smiled. She knew she had made the right choice, and having the train leave at such a convenient time only confirmed it. "How much is the ticket?" she asked.

"One dollar and forty-five cents," the clerk replied.

Emily handed over her silver dollar and two of her three quarters, and received a nickel and a ticket. "Track on the right," the clerk said.

Emily put the nickel in her pocket and clutched the ticket. No one seemed to notice her or to care that she was dressed in an Austen uniform. She had the money for a ticket, and that made it all right.

The train arrived a few minutes later. Emily boarded it nervously. She had taken the train twice before in her life, once when her father died and Aunt Mabel came to get her, and again when the Dowlings had taken her to the orphan home, but she had never ridden one alone. Then again, she had never been a runaway before. She had never even met her sister before. This was a day for firsts, and she told herself she could handle them.

"Will you announce when we get to Longview?" she asked the conductor when he punched her ticket.

"I sure will, young lady," he replied. "I'll say it nice and clear so you'll be certain to hear me."

"Thank you," she said. The train was only half full, and she found a seat by a window. It was exciting watching the scenery as the train took her away from the orphan home and toward her new family.

It was late morning when the train reached Longview. The conductor called the name of the town right in front of Emily's seat, and she smiled her thanks at him. "Have a pleasant day, young lady," he said to her as she got off the train.

"I'm going to," she said. "I'm going to have the best day of my life."

"That's the spirit," he said.

Emily looked around the train station, trying to figure out what to do next. She'd written the letter to the Smileys herself, but Miss Alice had addressed the envelope, and all she knew was that the family lived on the outskirts of town. She didn't know Mr. or Mrs. Smiley's first name. She didn't even know her sister's first name.

Her sister was sure to be in school, Emily thought, so school was the logical place to find her. She began walking left from the train station, and within a few blocks, she located a school.

It was a small red brick building, much smaller than the school in Oakbridge. There was a playground in the front and Emily saw young children running around.

She walked over to the playground, trying to appear casual, but terrified that some grown-up would confront her and question her appearance. There was a teacher outside supervising the children, but she was busy breaking up a fight and paid no attention to Emily.

Emily was confident her sister would somehow instantly know it was she, if they could only see each other. She glanced quickly at the children in the yard, looking for a beautiful little girl with long blond curls.

There were several little girls that looked just as she imagined her sister, but when Emily checked them more carefully, she realized they were all younger than eight. Her sister must be inside the school building.

Emily's stomach rumbled. It would be lunchtime soon, she realized, and there was a good chance that at lunchtime all the children were allowed to go to the yard and play. She decided that all she had to do was wait, and then she would be sure to see her sister.

Emily found a bench near enough to the school that she could keep an eye on it. She sat there and imagined the moment, only minutes away, she was sure, when she and her sister would recognize each other.

There would be quite a commotion when that happened. It would be a happy one for all to see. Mr. and Mrs. Smiley would undoubtedly be informed, and they'd come to the school and share in the joy of the reunion. Then they'd take both their daughters home with them, and Emily would move into their big home, with a pony and a cat, and most importantly a piano.

To keep herself from getting too excited, Emily practiced her fingering. Today she would play only happy music for herself and her new family.

"And what are you doing on this bench, young lady?"

Emily looked up and saw a policeman staring down at her.

"Shouldn't you be in school," the policeman asked, "instead of sunning yourself on this fine autumn day?"

Emily tried not to give in to her panic. If she didn't give the policeman just the right answer, she might never see her sister. "I'm looking for Mr. Smiley," she answered.

"You're not likely to find him on this bench," the policeman said.

"Do you know where he is?" Emily asked.

"I might," the policeman replied. "If you should happen to tell me why you're looking for him."

"My mother asked me to," Emily said. "She most particularly wants me to see his daughter."

"Then it's Mr. Ralph Smiley you'd be wanting to see," the policeman said. "Mr. Joseph Smiley has only sons."

"Yes, Mr. Ralph Smiley," Emily said. "He has a daughter, about eight years old."

"That he has," the policeman said. "Since you're so eager to meet the man, I'll escort you myself to his office."

"Thank you," Emily said. That wasn't the way she imagined the reunion, but she was in no position to argue with the policeman. She got off the bench and walked with the officer several blocks through town. She was sure everybody was looking at them. Someday, she told herself, the Smileys would laugh at the story of how Emily first came to live with them.

"Mr. Smiley's office is on the second floor of this building," the policeman said. Emily looked up, and saw RALPH SMILEY, ATTORNEY-AT-LAW painted on the outside of the second-story window.

"I'll walk up the stairs with you," the policeman said. "No point losing you right now."

"Yes, sir," Emily said. She was only a few feet

away, she told herself. Keep calm and soon things will work out just the way they're supposed to.

The policeman opened the office door. A nicely dressed woman was sitting at a desk.

"This young lady wishes to see Mr. Smiley," the policeman said. "Would the gentleman be free to see her?"

"I'll find out," the lady said. "Who shall I say wishes to see him?"

"Emily Lathrop Hasbrouck," Emily answered.

"Very well," the lady said. "Wait here." She entered an inner office, and quite a few minutes later, came back out. "Mr. Smiley will see you," she told Emily. "Thank you very much, Officer, for bringing her here. Mr. Smiley says there's no need for you to stay any longer."

Emily wished she didn't feel quite so dirty. She wished her hair had grown out more. She wished Mr. Smiley would rush out to greet her. But instead she walked alone into his office.

"You're Emily Hasbrouck?" Mr. Smiley asked. He was an older man, heavy and nearly bald. He didn't look anything like how Emily had imagined him.

"Yes, sir," Emily said, telling herself not to judge by appearances. "Emily Lathrop Hasbrouck. Did you get my letter?"

"Oh, yes, I got it," Mr. Smiley said. "I have it right here. My wife and I preferred not to keep it at our house."

"Oh," Emily said. She was sure Mr. Smiley

had a good reason. "Then you know I've come to meet my sister. You know my father died, and so did my aunt Mabel, and my sister is the only family I have left." She tried to smile, but it felt false. "My mother would want the two of us to be together."

"Your mother is dead eight years now," Mr. Smiley said. "And to the best of my knowledge, she expressed no deathbed wishes on the subject of you at all."

"She meant to," Emily said. "I'm sure she would have if she'd known my father was going to die, and then Aunt Mabel. She would have wanted me to live with my sister. She wouldn't have wanted me to live in an orphanage." She hoped she could keep the desperation out of her voice. She wished Mr. Smiley would at least tell her to sit down. None of this was going the way she'd imagined.

"Your story is a very sad one," Mr. Smiley said. "But it's of no concern to me. When your mother died, your father renounced all rights to his infant daughter, and my wife and I adopted her. She is not a Hasbrouck. She's been a Smiley since she was one week old. She has a mother and a father and no sisters."

"But when you got my letter," Emily said. "You must have told her about me then. Doesn't she know I'm coming?"

"She has no knowledge of you," Mr. Smiley said. "She does not even know she's adopted, and my wife and I intend to keep it that way at any cost."

"But I'm her sister," Emily said. "I'm her flesh and blood."

Mr. Smiley stared at her. Emily felt so weak, she had to hold on to his desk to keep from sinking into the floor. "You are not her sister," he said. "Legally my daughter has no sisters. Her life began the moment she was adopted. It wouldn't matter if she had a thousand sisters, or if your Auntie Mabel were still alive, or even your drunkard father. My daughter is as much a Smiley as if she'd been born one, and nothing you can say will ever change that."

"But I can be a Smiley too," Emily said. "You could adopt me also. She'd like that. I'm sure she would. I'd be a wonderful big sister to her."

Mr. Smiley laughed. "Don't be a fool," he said. "My wife and I know how lucky we are that our daughter is a decent child. She was born in wedlock, but we took our chances when we brought her home. At my insistence, we have always been quite strict with her and she has yet to show any signs of hereditary weakness. But we're hardly about to take in a guttersnipe like you."

Emily swallowed hard. She couldn't give up hope. Not yet. "All right, then," she said. "I won't be a Smiley. I won't even tell her we're sisters. But let me work for you at least. Let me be your housemaid. I'm a good worker, honest, I am. Give me that much of a home, please."

"I know all about you," Mr. Smiley said, "and you disgust me. I know what kind of miserable deceitful being you are."

"What are you talking about?" Emily asked.

"My wife and I had no knowledge of what had become of you, nor did we care," Mr. Smiley said. "The past eight years we never once thought about you. We were informed through our friends when your father died, but what became of you was no concern to us. Frankly, we were relieved when we learned of his death, since that meant he would make no effort to extort money from us in exchange for our daughter. He seemed to me the type that would, if he ever sobered up enough to come up with the scheme."

"He wasn't like that," Emily said. "He was a good man."

"I didn't give you permission to speak," Mr. Smiley said. "As I was saying, Mrs. Smiley and I barely remembered your existence, until you sent us that unfortunate letter. We discussed what we should do about it, until I remembered that my friend Judge Cosgrove sits on the board of trustees at Austen. I telephoned him and he read to me your letter of apology to his daughter for the incident in which you assaulted her and her crippled friend."

"It didn't happen that way," Emily said. "I was made to write that letter."

Mr. Smiley ignored her. "Just now, when I found you were in my office, I called the Austen

Home to inform them that you had run away. Miss Browne seemed unduly concerned, and I gathered immediately you were in serious trouble. When she refused to tell me what was going on, I telephoned Judge Cosgrove. He told me of your false accusations against his daughter and her friends."

"They weren't false," Emily said. "Isabella Cosgrove and Harriet pushed Gracie, and that's why she died."

"Judge Cosgrove informs me that the Austen Home is a model institution," Mr. Smiley said. "Of course, no orphanage can be better than its wards, but he says the girls there are all fed well and wear decent clothing and are taught their proper place in society. Apparently they were most reluctant to take you in because of your age, but strings were pulled and exceptions were most regrettably made. When the judge learned that you had run away today, he agreed with me that you didn't deserve to live at the Austen Home. He has undoubtedly already spoken to Miss Browne and informed her of his decision."

"But where will I go?" Emily asked.

"That is not my concern," Mr. Smiley said. "Understand that if I ever see you in Longview again, I'll have you arrested for extortion. Just because you're a child doesn't mean you can't be locked up for many years when you are guilty of such a grievous crime. In fact, because you are so young, there would be no need for a trial. You're a ward of the court already. A judge's order is all that's required to have you sent away."

Trying to hold back her tears, Emily managed to say, "I'm sorry. I'm sorry about everything. Please don't send me to jail."

"Very well," Mr. Smiley said. "You understand you are never to return to Longview? You are never to make any attempt to contact any member of my family, myself, my wife, or my daughter?"

"I understand what you're saying," Emily said.

"Should I find that you have, I will see to it that you are locked up in an institution for many years," Mr. Smiley said. "In addition, I will have to become that much stricter to my daughter, to ensure that she does not fall into the wicked ways that are unfortunately her biological inheritance. My wife is quite softhearted when it comes to that child, but she defers to me when it comes to issues of discipline. Do I make myself understood? Not only would you suffer from any further attempts to contact us, but I would be forced to be even more severe in the discipline of my daughter as well."

"Oh, no," Emily said. "Don't hurt her because of me, I beg you."

"Very well," Mr. Smiley said. "Do you solemnly vow you will make no further effort to contact by letter or visit any member of my family, myself, my wife, or my daughter?"

"I solemnly vow," Emily said. Her voice trembled from the effort to keep from crying. "Just don't hurt her. None of this is her fault. It's mine, not hers. Don't punish her because of me."

"We have nothing further to discuss," Mr. Smiley said. "I'll drive you in my automobile a few miles out of town. If you choose, you may make your way back to Oakbridge. I'm sure Judge Cosgrove and Miss Browne have made arrangements for your transfer elsewhere. It's no concern of mine where you end up, just as long as I never see or hear from you again."

"I swear to you, you never will," Emily said. "Just don't hurt her."

✢ Chapter 12

Mr. Smiley left his office and led Emily out to his automobile. Emily sat beside him, and willed herself not to cry as they drove away from Longview, from her sister. Mr. Smiley made no effort to speak to her and Emily knew well enough to keep silent.

After a half hour or so, Mr. Smiley pulled the automobile over to the side of the road. "Get out," he said.

"Yes, sir," Emily said. She climbed out from the seat, and stood there as Mr. Smiley turned the automobile around toward Longview. It threw dirt all over her as she stood there.

Emily felt one tear run down her cheek, then another, until soon she was crying uncontrollably. She hid behind a tree, then sank down onto the ground, and wept all the tears she had locked inside her, tears of rage and loss for Gracie, tears of sorrow and terror for herself and her future. She cried harder than she had since the death of her father. When at long last she felt no more tears inside her, she wiped the now dampened dirt off her face, got up, and began her walk away from Longview.

Oakbridge had to be at least thirty miles away, Emily realized. Not that there was much point going back there. But she truly didn't know where else to go.

Emily mocked herself as she began the long walk back. Who was she to think she had a place in this world? Her mother was weak to have ever married a Hasbrouck, and her father was a drunkard, just as everyone said, and she was a no-good sinner, not even grateful to Aunt Mabel for taking her in and saving her from the streets. Now she was paying for her sins. She deserved no better than what she had, no home, no family, no friends, no money. Whatever gave her the right to think that just because her sister had been adopted by good people, she belonged with them as well? She should have been grateful to be placed at the Austen Home. She had known what the alternatives were, yet it wasn't good enough for her. No, she was a Lathrop, and Lathrops deserved better than three meals a day and a roof over their heads. They deserved pretty dresses and piano lessons and the right to walk on sidewalks. What a fool she was. A wicked, sinful fool. It would serve her right if no one took her in and she was forced into begging. It would serve her right if she starved to death. At least then her sister would never have to worry that she'd be punished for something Emily had done.

Emily realized with a start that she still didn't know her sister's name or what she looked like. To think Emily had dared to dream of a home with her, of sharing in her love. Her sister didn't know she existed, and now she would never know, any more than Emily would know her name.

Emily realized then how Mary Kate must feel, completely alone, completely abandoned. She had no more family than Mary Kate, no more chance of a home. Gracie at least had had the dream of a family. Mary Kate had nothing she didn't make for herself. No wonder she left when Gracie died. What did she have to stay for?

She was going to miss Mary Kate, Emily realized. The one thing Oakbridge had given her was friends, Mary Kate and Gracie, Miss Alice and Aunt Bessie.

Of course, Miss Alice and Aunt Bessie weren't true friends. They were just kindly people who'd taken pity on her. Emily had been a fool to think they cared any more about her than Aunt Mabel's friends had. After all, Miss Alice had a career, and a marriage to look forward to. Aunt Bessie had a job as well, and family. Emily was a recipient of their charity, as many other people undoubtedly had been. But she couldn't count on them. She wasn't their friend or their servant. She meant no more to them than a tramp they'd give a free meal to. It was just like her to read more into their kindness than that.

Emily then forced herself to think of Gracie. All weekend long she'd tried not to, to prevent herself from self-reproach. But now it didn't matter. She couldn't feel any lower than she did at that moment. She might as well hate herself for Gracie's death.

But she couldn't picture Gracie angry at her. Gracie was angry at Harriet and Isabella and Florrie for being cruel to her, for pushing her into the street. They were the reasons why Gracie died, not Emily. Even if Emily had done as Gracie had asked, and refused to walk in the street, the others still would have been angry and still would have pushed them off the sidewalk. Maybe things would have been different. Maybe she would have been the one to fall against the rock and die. Maybe Gracie would have been a few inches farther along and not hit her head. But Emily couldn't have predicted what was going to happen. She didn't kill Gracie, and she couldn't have kept her from being killed either.

Harriet and Isabella killed Gracie. It was that simple. They didn't mean to, but they were responsible nonetheless.

Emily stood absolutely still. She had nothing, she now knew, but having nothing had its advantages. Before she was terrified of being sent to a city orphanage because that would have meant miserable conditions. She was terrified of being sent to jail because that would have meant the Smileys wouldn't take her in. Well, she had no chance of playing the piano ever again, and no chance of being adopted by the Smileys. Having lost everything, she had nothing left to lose.

She couldn't save Gracie's life, but that didn't mean she didn't owe her something. All Gracie wanted was to walk on the sidewalk, to be treated with the same respect as anybody else. That really wasn't very much. It wasn't a family or piano lessons or pretty yellow dresses. It was no more than Gracie's due, no more than anybody's, really. There were no laws forbidding orphans and foundlings from walking on the sidewalk. There were no laws permitting people to push them off.

Emily stood absolutely still and stared ahead at the long road. She would never make it to Oakbridge by foot that day, and with only thirty cents, she had no other way of getting there. It would take two, maybe three days of hard walking before she got there, and the thirty cents would have to buy her all the food she could count on eating. She wasn't going to beg from strangers for a meal or a place to sleep. But she was determined to get to Oakbridge. She owed it to Gracie to tell people the truth. Now, more than ever, she realized, although she couldn't be quite sure why, that she owed it to herself.

Automobiles and buggies passed her as she

walked, but no one stopped to offer her a ride. She didn't care. The longer she walked, the angrier she got. And she didn't care that anger was a sin either. She was a sinner, but she sure wasn't the only one she knew. Let someone else pay for his sins for a change.

Emily was hungry and exhausted and consumed with rage as she trudged toward Oakbridge. She was so tired, so lost in her thoughts, she didn't notice that an automobile coming her way had slowed to a stop.

"Emily! Emily!"

She heard her name and looked up.

It was Miss Alice.

"Emily. Thank God, I found you. Get into the automobile."

Emily did what she was told. "How did you find me?" she asked.

"When Mr. Smiley called Austen, my mother listened in," Miss Alice said. "She listened to his conversation with Judge Cosgrove also. Oh, Emily. I'm so sorry about everything."

"Harriet and Isabella killed Gracie," Emily said. "I don't care if anybody believes me. I don't care if they send me to jail for saying so. That's what happened. I know. I was there. I saw them do it."

"I believe you," Miss Alice said. "And I've already spoken to the police and to the newspaper. As soon as I learned what had happened, I reported what I had seen, how Harriet and the oth-

151

ers had tormented you. One of the policemen believes you as well. Gracie wouldn't have crossed that street if she were running back to the Home. It's in the opposite direction. The policeman wants to talk to you, Emily, and hear your version of what happened. I can't guarantee there'll be justice for Gracie. The Dales and the Cosgroves and the Sheldons are powerful people. But if you tell the truth, I'll back you up, and just maybe we'll be able to do something."

"I owe it to Gracie," Emily said.

"We all owe it to Gracie," Miss Alice said. "She lived in Oakbridge. She was one of ours. She deserves justice."

Emily was silent for a moment. She pictured Gracie, and she made her a solemn vow to tell the truth about the way she'd died, regardless of the consequences. "I can't go back to Austen," she said. "They won't let me in."

"My mother told me," Miss Alice said. "You'll stay with us, at least until all this gets resolved."

"I can earn my keep," Emily said. "I know Mrs. Macdonald does day-work for you, but there's still plenty I can do. I'm not going to take your charity anymore."

"Oh, Emily," Miss Alice said. "We've never given you charity."

"You fed me," Emily said. "You let me play your piano."

"We did that because we like you," Miss Alice said. "We think of you as our friend."

"I don't deserve to be your friend," Emily said. "I've never deserved friends. I'm guilty of covetousness and vanity and anger. I'm a terrible sinner."

"Emily, we're all sinners," Miss Alice said. "God doesn't expect us to be perfect. He just wants us to try to be the best possible people we can be. You have just as much right to friends and family and a good life as anybody else, and don't you ever forget it."

Emily heard Miss Alice's words and knew they were true, yet tears streamed down her face as she stared out the front of the automobile. "I want justice for Gracie. I want to go to school. I want to play the piano." She bit her lip. "I want somebody to love me. I don't want to be alone."

Miss Alice put her arm around Emily. "Somebody does love you," she said. "I do, and my mother does. You'll never be alone as long as people love you. Just stay by my side, Emily. Now, let me turn this automobile around and I'll take us home."